PIRATE'S PLUNDER

STEPHANIE FLYNN

Small Fish Publishing
USA

First edition
Cover design by Stephanie Flynn
ISBN eBook: 978-1-952372-51-3
ISBN paperback: 978-1-952372-50-6
ISBN hardcover: 978-1-952372-54-4
ISBN large print paperback: 978-1-952372-68-1

Also By Stephanie Flynn

Find my catalog at StephanieFlynn.com
Immortal Protector series
0.5 Vampire's Distraction
1 Vampire's Deception
2 Vampire's Secret
3 Vampire's Promise
3.5 Elf Bound
4 Vampire's Demand

Immortal Protector Side Tales
Deer Holiday
Love Claws
Depths of the Heart

Matchmaker in Time series
0.5 Minutes to Live

1 Seconds to Act
2 Hours to Arrive
3 Days to Hide
4 Years to Savor

Pirates in Time series
1 Pirate's Prize
2 Pirate's Treasure
3 Pirate's Plunder

Time Travel Romance Shorts
Fateful Time
One Crazy Time

If you like your urban fantasy without the romance, too, check out Stephanie Flynn's other name, Marie Flynn!

Special Note

While the events of this novel are fiction, the pirate raid on Gambia Castle was real, performed by Captain Howell Davis in 1718.

Chapter 1

ROBIN HALL SPREAD HER legs apart and leaned forward. Nerves tightened her stomach. It had been too long since she'd worked up the courage to do this. To be here. Focus. She gazed through the sight to her target. Aim for the heart. Aim for the kill. This man would not hesitate to take her out first. The rapid pops around her penetrated her hearing protection, but she didn't lose her focus.

Her index finger shifted into position. This time, she would prevail. Robin took up the trigger slack. Breathe in. Breathe out. Now or never. Tensing her arms, she squeezed off round after round in a rapid succession at her enemy. First at the heart. Then at the head. Between the eyes. No mistakes.

Pop, pop, pop.

Behind her eye protection, she blinked with each squeeze, but she focused like her life depended on it. Robin channeled her anger and pain at the target, ensuring he couldn't be a threat any longer.

Life wasn't fair—she'd been exposed to that lesson early on. Robin had tripped during a race and skinned her knee, causing her to lose. She was six years old at the time, but Robin wasn't capable of truly understanding. As a teenager, a devastating mistake had Robin questioning that lesson all over again. Her life had been torn from her, and through the pain and therapy, Robin tried to understand the 'why' of it. She never got any satisfying answers.

One by one, Robin unloaded the rounds. Her arms trembled with the recoil until the magazine emptied. Robin lowered the weapon and blew out a deep breath. She pressed the button alongside the partition to pull her target paper forward.

Direct hits to the head and chest. She counted the holes—no misses. There was nothing physically wrong with her aim. There was nothing wrong with her at all, but two people died because she froze up when it mattered most.

"Not bad for a rookie," Detective Todd Blenny said, reaching out for her target and tearing it off the hanger. He wore a suit, and he filled it out well. Too bad the insides didn't match the outsides.

"I'm not a rookie," Robin said sharply and removed her protective gear. Robin had dawdled in private security for years, strolling the properties of slumbering corporate assets, until she was finally accepted into the police academy a few months ago—her dream ever since that fatal mistake when she was a teenager.

But most of the city's police department treated her like she was still green. When she'd screwed up royally, and she'd been assigned to weeks of administrative leave for the investigation, she'd deserved their ridicule. Now she was back, and she just proved she was capable. No more mistakes. Robin couldn't live with another life lost on her account.

Blenny stuffed a finger through one of the holes. "I didn't think you could do this."

Robin had passed the academy's rigorous training. Of course she could. Without a rebuttal, Robin left the indoor shooting range, passing through the corridor of offices, but Blenny followed on her tail. If there was ever a proverbial 'wolf in sheep's clothing', Blenny's face would be under the definition.

"I meant to say welcome back," he called from behind her.

The words rang hollow. Blenny didn't want her on the force, none of her colleagues did. The unspoken truth was plain on their faces, and the snark and murmurs whispering through the office made their thoughts far more obvious. Even quiet Jessica, the front desk officer, cast her glares while making copies.

Several weeks ago, Robin had responded to an active shooter situation outside a bank, and when she needed to eliminate the hostile, she froze. Officer Clark Thompson took a round to the femoral and bled out, but *he* stopped the shooter. He was a hero.

Robin was the incompetent enemy still lurking among them. She'd needed that leave to recollect herself, reflect, and figure out where she'd gone wrong, and her colleagues needed even longer to rebuild that trust. But they didn't know Robin hadn't figured out where she'd gone wrong, and she'd convinced the department's shrink she had a handle on her mistake. Robin needed to redeem herself, so she'd lied.

Returning to the practice range today was the first step in figuring out why she'd failed to save Clark Thompson. It wasn't her aim.

Her response to Blenny was superficial and dry. "Thanks."

"So, can we make it a date? I'm free Friday night." Blenny held the door open for her.

Robin ducked under his thick arm with growing irritation at his tired request. "I already said no."

"I've heard of the mystical women who can subsist entirely on their man-eating thoughts, but I never saw one in person." He paused and quirked a sassy smile, attempting to provoke Robin into conversing with him.

Robin ignored him, passing by neat rows of desks with stacked files and humming computers. People moved around; always busy.

"Is this about the shooting? Look, you and me, we're okay. I wanted to take you out long before that, and it didn't change things for me."

It changed a lot of things for her. Blenny was the only cheerleader on her side, but for only one reason. Robin sat behind her desk and woke her screen. She asked dryly, "Would you like some pom-poms?"

The brute of a man leaned down into her personal space. "Come on. You gave Riggs and Angry Boston a chance. We both like food, right? I'll drive."

She had gone on a date with each of them once, before her incident, as the shrink called it, but neither of those dates ended well. The difference was she, Riggs, and Angry Boston had mutual interest. Robin could see through Blenny's crap, and she was never making the mistake of dating within the office again. "I'm busy."

Blenny laughed. "I don't buy that. You live alone, and you're an only child. Your mom passed away, and your dad is unknown. Your friends are those pathetic cretins at the Value SuperMart, probably working on a Friday night, whereas you and I aren't pathetic or working that night."

He rattled off her entire life's situation in a string of statements, each a verbal slap to the face. She knew her friends were all she had. Blenny didn't need to remind her.

Robin gripped the edge of her desk until her knuckles blanched, trying to hold back the reaction he fished for. "That information is none of your business, and you can't use departmental resources for your personal snooping."

After all that transpired in a short period of time, Robin wasn't going to stick around long enough to vest in her pension. She didn't want to let down her mom, but Robin couldn't stay here any longer.

"I'm messing with you, Hall. If you're truly busy on Friday, then I'll pick you up on Saturday," Blenny said softly.

Robin pressed her lips into a tight smile. "I'm busy all weekend. The answer is no. Now please allow me to do my job."

A detective in a navy blue suit pressed a file against Blenny's tie. "This one just came in. Lieutenant wants us to spearhead."

"Let's wrap this one up quick. I have plans this weekend." Blenny sent her what was probably a flirty smile and strutted away, matching stride with his partner on the case.

Robin exhaled in relief at the break. She'd wanted to move away to a small town, where no one knew her. A place where break-ins weren't commonplace. Where a murder didn't sit unsolved for years because of too little resources and too many dead ends. A place where bad memories wouldn't haunt her. After a festival this weekend with her favorite *pathetic cretins*, Robin was going to spend the rest of her spare-time job hunting. She didn't fit in as an officer.

She hoped Emily and Angela showed up this weekend. The outfit Angela had chosen for Robin made her skin crawl, but the woman assured her Robin would fit right in. That she could handle.

Robin didn't want Blenny seeing it, or anyone else on the force who already made up their minds about her.

2

Chapter 2

Nassau, New Providence Island, Bahamas, 1715

CAPTAIN NOAH RILEY SIPPED an indistinguishable liquid from his mug at the best tavern in town, the renowned Golden Macaw. Part ale, part punch, and a splash or several of rum—whatever it was, the liquor was hardly palatable. But he sipped the concoction slowly, so as not to raise concern amid the chorus of celebratory laughter.

Half his crew slammed empty mugs on thick oak tables, calling out for refills. The other half already buried themselves in the arms of the brothel next door. After their latest prize of Spanish gold from Cuba, the now-wealthy men deserved a shore leave—their first in weeks. The former *Sea Lion* and current *Angelfish* crew knew how to spend their money, and the funds dwindled with efficiency, which was fine.

A pirate's career was shorter than the average man's, so the captain's only goal was to find a prize to satisfy the crew and break up the account. Each day toiling at sea increased their risk of finding that short end: hanging by the neck until dead under King George's gibbet.

A risk Riley was comfortable taking.

Riley had never asked to become their leader, nor had he challenged the previous captain for the position, but as a dangerous situation unfolded with Spain on their last account, Riley had threatened to take the captaincy, should the foolish—but lucky—Captain Henry Price fail. It was a hollow threat; he'd never expected to follow through. But that was the precise moment he began to wonder. And now, at six-and-twenty years of age, Noah Riley was captain—elected unanimously.

As the *Angelfish* had hove to in the protected bay of Nassau to resupply, refit, and to give the crew its much-needed shore leave. Riley spent his time narrowing down his plan for the account, and Nassau's fort taunted him with its reinforced walls, range of artillery, and continuous defense by armed men.

He wouldn't dare raid the defenses of their pirate home, but as he'd studied it and picked the brains of sailors coming and going, Riley had decided on his target. This one would solve the crew's money problems for life and bring Riley back to his family. It was perfect.

Incredibly dangerous, but Riley didn't care. He swirled the liquid in his mug, avoiding its flavor.

"Captain, have another round with us. We're paying!" Buckley, the master carpenter, said, lifting a full mug and grinning with fewer teeth than customary. The old man brushed aside his black shoulder-length hair, the gray temples only appearing once in a while. The experienced man was dedicated to the sea, and although his aim with a hammer left everyone wanting, Buckley was dependable and willing to put the crew in their places should the need arise. He'd make a great quartermaster, but Buckley had always refused.

On their last account, Buckley had come within moments of the aforementioned gibbet. The carpenter had always said hanging by the throat was the worst way to die. Displaying a man's body in a spectacle was shameful in the worst way.

Riley figured once a man was dead, he no longer cared, so any shame was carried by the living. But Riley never voiced that opinion, lest the crew became suspicious.

A woman who'd appeared on their ship under Captain Price's leadership saved Buckley and many of the crew from that fate, including Captain Price himself. Riley still couldn't believe a woman had that much power and strength, but he hadn't been there.

"Come on, captain," Buckley pressed.

On an island full of ruffians and thieves, one could never be too careful with valuable information. As much as he trusted his crew, the drink tended to cause loose lips, and he'd kept his plans close to the chest for that reason. But apparently Riley had ignored his drink too long, and the crew noticed. "I haven't finished this one yet, but you go ahead. I insist."

Riley sipped to prove his word.

The carpenter patted him on the shoulder and gestured for his own refill. "Lighten up, captain. The day is young, and the rum is endless!"

Crew on the other side of him cheered the man's declaration, and Buckley chatted with them, leaving Riley alone.

But not for long.

Riley rubbed his thumb against the mug's handle, and the gangly William Price approached on sea legs, carrying his own sloshing drink. Riley smiled at the previous captain's brother, once presumed dead but rescued by that same woman. The only explanation Riley could swallow was witchcraft. How else could a woman perform such impossible feats?

If they were true at all.

Even with ample provisions since the rescue, William Price had never regained his healthful shape. Although Captain Henry Price retired from the sea with his impossible woman, William insisted on staying, claiming the domestic life wasn't for him, and with his history, Riley was happy to have him.

Price rested a hand on Riley's shoulder for balance and dropped onto a stool next to him. "I was chained in the hold of the *Peibo del ler San Francisco* for months. As much as I love the leisure time with the women, I want to see the open ocean again. What's the next move, captain? Any exciting leads?"

"Yea, we can't stay here forever," Cantu said, taking up the chair next to the armorer. The wood groaned under his heft of thick, corded muscle. Cantu was a highly regarded man on the crew. Trustworthy. Loyal to the articles. Strong as a tree and built like an elephant. A true asset to any crew, and he'd been with them since Riley first tasted the sea. "The musician is on the verge of pawning his violin soon, and I never saw a man drink as much as the boatswain. If Karl's not broke yet, he will be tomorrow."

"That man better slow down or he'll be begging for scraps," Buckley said, laughing. "Barkeep! Another fill!"

"Cantu has a point," Price said. "Some of us need another prize. Not that I'm ungrateful for our noteworthy luck thus far."

Riley couldn't keep their next target a secret forever, and since they were weighing anchor later this afternoon word couldn't spread fast enough to foil their plans, and since he needed full cooperation to pull off the incredible feat, Riley said, "Fort James."

"What about it?" Price smiled, crinkling the corners of his eyes, reminding Riley of the younger Price. As much as they'd fought in recent weeks, Riley missed his old captain, his friend.

Riley sipped from his mug and winced as he swallowed. "We're going to take it."

Price laughed. "I know I'm three sheets to the wind when I hear such preposterous words. What did you say?"

"What's preposterous?" Buckley asked, belching his approval of the rum-like concoction.

Riley had expected resistance. Pirates were thieves, but they weren't foolish. "We're going to raid the English fort on the Gambia River."

The men stared.

Price chugged down the rest of his mug and slammed the empty on the bar. "It may as well be called a fortified castle. Gun batteries line the perimeter. Soldiers number in the dozens, if not hundreds. If we're ambushed, the sheer cliffs on either side of the river mean we have no escape. There's no way we can succeed in taking her."

"Taking who?" John Randall, the new quartermaster, who'd also been rescued from the *San Francisco* by Price's woman, appeared on Riley's other side, thumbs hanging on his sash. He was well qualified for the job, but Riley didn't know where he sat with the man. All that mattered was the crew trusted him and voted for him.

"We're raiding a fort," Price answered for him, lifting his empty for a refill. "Going to need more rum for this one."

"A fort?" Randall asked. "That's a higher risk than we usually take on. What's the prize worth?"

Everything. "Enough for each man to say goodbye to the sea forever, if he chose."

Cantu shifted his weight, creaking the chair once again, and spoke in jovial celebration. "Why is it you want to retire us? Aren't we a good enough family?"

Riley hoped their excessive drinking and teasing would make them forget the question, but alas, they quieted down and waited for Riley to answer. On a sigh, he said, "I want you to have the freedom to choose."

"We love the sea," Cantu said. "She was made for us. Karl and Jack Watts would agree, too, if their arms weren't elbow deep in whore right now."

The men laughed, and drink sloshed over their mugs. Some rained down on Riley, and he frowned. Washing clothes was nigh impossible on the ship, but still plenty difficult on land, and these were his best garments.

In their stories, the crew mentioned a few others enjoying the brothel: Giles, the portly cook, which surprised everyone, and little Peter Gunner, which surprised no one. The men wanted to spoil the young man, as Riley had been at his age. Hodgens was apparently over there, too, but he refrained from participating, no matter how much Karl flaunted the flesh before him.

Randall's eyes glinted with greed, and he rose his voice to drown out the storytelling. "For one, I don't care why. My concern is, do we have the men for it?"

The crew quieted down, listening with growing interest. Price drank from his refilled mug. Cantu shook his head in the negative.

"I'm with Cantu on this one," McKee said, lifting his bald head above the others to be heard. Ale glistened on his scraggly beard, but no matter his rough appearance, the master gunner was a loyal man. "We need at least twenty more men. With the other crews roaming the island right now, finding enough free agents willing to sign is going to leave us scraping the bottom of the barrel."

Riley's men numbered a dozen from the original lot, and another dozen who were rescued and agreed to join the account. But to take a fortified castle, they did need more. "Randall, as quartermaster, I task you with recruiting. Make sure the hands are experienced."

"Consider it done," Randall said. "After I finish my next round. Barkeeper!"

Riley smiled and pushed his mug toward his quartermaster. "Take mine. I need air."

Buckley laughed. "Another round, men, then it's our turn at the brothel!"

The crew cheered.

3

Chapter 3

THIS WAS A MISTAKE. A huge mistake. One she would bury in the fathomless depths of her mind for all eternity. If anyone dared speak of it, she would vanish in embarrassment. Robin covered her thighs with her purse, attempting to shield herself against the gawkers—who were dressed as normal people. Why had she listened to Angela and Emily? They'd both said the festival-goers would be dressed in pirate-y wear. The few here and there were vastly outnumbered by people wearing pants.

Robin was not.

Angela Foxe told her which costume in a bag to buy—the exact same one as Angela's. Something about sexy twin pirates. Robin didn't know anything about this stuff. The ivory blouse was rimmed in ruffles, and the length of the dress was uneven—on purpose, Angela had said. The brown corset on the outside was restrictive, and there was nowhere in this outfit for her to conceal-carry, so she left her weapon at home.

Along with her dignity.

Where were Angela and Emily? They were supposed to meet her here, and as far as Robin was concerned, there was safety in numbers. Right now, she was the lone gazelle, and the cheetahs eyeing her like a tasty meal made her eye twitch. Robin pulled out her cell phone, pretending to be busy, and tried to hide her blushing hot face.

Robin sent them both a text. '*I'm here. Where are you?*'

A cell phone chimed nearby, and Robin turned her head in anticipation of joining her lost herd, but she didn't recognize the man eagerly checking his phone. Robin sighed and texted, '*I was at your store yesterday picking up a shoplifter, but you were both at lunch. Sorry I missed you.*'

She waited a beat and put away her phone.

Down the grassy hill, rows of tented vendors sold refreshments, gear, and trinkets for the enthusiasts. To the right, along the dock, was a single tall ship, about to set sail. And into the Bay of Green Bay—the large swath of water connected to Lake Michigan—another tall ship was returning to shore with tourists.

Knowing Emily's obsession with pirates, Robin's friends didn't wait once the ships were ready to sail, and they wouldn't have a cell signal way out there. Robin shielded her eyes from the sun and scanned the festival grounds, looking for something—someone—comforting.

Security. There had to be security on the grounds. She'd talk shop and network, and if the situation called for it, she'd assist while off-duty, especially with those ancient boats being the draw of the day. How sturdy were those old ships, anyway? Was the Coast Guard on standby in case one took on water and sunk? Robin didn't like boats at all. The last time she'd boarded a pleasure boat, it ended terribly, making her that much more fearful of boats in general, but especially ancient ones. Even though she could swim, she liked keeping her feet on dry ground.

Robin didn't see any security station or any uniformed officers roaming the festival. There had to be someone.

"Hall? Is that you?" Blenny's unwanted voice penetrated her eardrums, and a skitter of nerves ran through her. *Someone, anyone, but Officer Blenny, please.*

Robin turned her head, gritting her teeth. Blenny, in sensible cargo shorts and a dark polo, leaned into her view, and his eyes roamed her outfit, lingering on her bare legs. Robin's back stiffened. It didn't take a genius for Blenny to learn one of her best friends was a nut for pirates, so Robin would be here.

"Stalking is illegal in all fifty states," she said dryly.

"And I didn't know you memorized all the laws applicable to each state. Color me impressed."

That was not her intent. Robin returned her purse to the front of her thighs. When she wore her uniform, she stood her ground, held her chin high. But wearing this? She was a self-conscious piece of meat.

She hated it.

"Have fun then," Robin said dismissively, coldness in her voice.

"Oh, I'm going to have fun," he said, staring at her exposed cleavage and miles of bare skin. Her chest didn't fill it out entirely, not like Angela, but the frilly lace and layers of polyester filled in where she was lacking.

A few weeks ago, Emily shared her progress on her own outfit, perfectly home-made and masculine. Robin wasn't into this scene, and therefore, not motivated to make her own costume—whether she'd decided on breeches or a skirt—so she trusted Angela's judgment on which costume in a bag to purchase. She wouldn't make that mistake again.

"Hold still. I need a picture." Blenny slipped his cell phone out of his back pocket.

"Absolutely not!"

This could not happen. She survived the work day despised by everyone; she couldn't stand to be a laughingstock.

"I only need a few seconds. Hold still."

"Leave me alone." Robin walked away. Hopefully he didn't choose to record a video instead, but she wasn't going to turn around to find out.

With Blenny left behind in her dust, Robin intended to make something from this bust of a day—one circle in good faith to find her friends and get credit for showing up. Then she was going home to put on soft clothing that covered her body, make a cup of hot cocoa, and binge watch television. Alone. After her eyeballs stung with sappy daytime drama, she planned on filling out applications, so there was no point in rocking the boat by complaining to the captain about Blenny's behavior.

Blenny, with a look of frustration, popped into her view again, slowing her steps. The humor had left his features. "You know what your problem is?"

Robin stared him down and stopped. "You're in my way."

"You didn't let Riggs or Angry Boston inside your apartment. I'd like to find out why." Blenny paused, groping her with his eyes.

Robin couldn't believe what he'd admitted. She wanted to slap him, but that would only encourage him further. She uttered a noise of disgust. "They shared details? With you?"

A mischievous grin split his face. "Everyone got all the details, so I know you must be so...*frustrated.* That's your problem."

His outrageous accusation was not only unfounded, but incredibly insulting and callous. Robin's mouth dropped open.

Blenny smirked. "Oh, I'm on the right track."

Robin tipped her chin up and marched around him, fighting back tears of humiliation. Not only did they hate her as an officer, but they didn't respect her as a person, either.

All she wanted was a man who could take care of himself and would cover her back, which after many failed relationships, fellow police officers sounded appealing, but that was clearly a non-starter. Based on experience, the trifecta of independent, strong, and *respectful* was as attainable as a magical unicorn. Six-year-old Robin was disappointed in learning the truth. Thirty-five-year-old Robin was only...

Relieved.

She was done hunting for her unicorn, a simple decision.

A freeing decision.

And this afternoon, Robin would begin the job hunt. Soon enough, she wouldn't have to face any of them again. Robin smiled to herself. Destiny called for her to become a crazy cat lady, and she would embrace it.

"I can fix your problem," Blenny called after her. "Think about it."

There's nothing about me that needs fixing.

Robin strolled by the vendors while scanning the festival grounds for her friends, or for anyone in need of assistance—any distraction from this craptastic day. Despite smiling about adopting a herd of cats, she would miss being an officer. Protecting people filled a need deep in her bones, and right now, that was all that kept her at this festival. With no security on staff and her friends incommunicado, Robin needed reassurance that everyone would remain safe. Although, if Blenny dropped over, clutching his chest, Robin *would* hesitate, wondering if he faked it for attention.

People conversed, laughed, and lounged on picnic tables with drinks in their hands. Others waited in line to buy food, which smelled like seared beef and oily fries. Other visitors took photos of themselves and some with strangers in costume. A few drank from bottles hidden in paper bags. Robin frowned at them, but since she was off duty, she let them be. With no real distractions here, Robin approached the vendor tables. The trinkets and food didn't interest her, but she stopped at a display of shiny swords. "Are these real?"

The vendor sitting behind the table wore a greasy stained apron around his thick waist. Lines on his face and cracks in his calloused hands suggested a lifetime of unparalleled craftmanship. The swords were real.

"Yes, ma'am. Handcrafted by the finest swordsmith this side of the snow belt. Be careful now; don't want to cut yourself, such a pretty thing like you." The gray-haired man smiled.

Robin pressed her lips together and walked away. She fished her phone out of her purse and checked the screen in case she'd left it muted or on vibrate.

No messages.

While walking, Robin texted them again. '*Guys, I'm by the vendors. Where are you? Still on a ship?*'

This time she waited a minute, but still neither replied. Robin had enough. She'd subjected herself to enough unwanted attention and embarrassment. Angela was going to hear about this, and Emily's sanity was going to be questioned.

Robin tucked her phone away and craned her neck to be sure Blenny wasn't behind her before she headed back his way toward the parking lot.

"Good morning, child." A woman's raspy voice stole Robin's attention.

She braced herself for more unwanted comments, but none came. Robin turned around and smiled politely. "Hi."

"See anything you like?" The withered woman stood up from a stool, her back hunched with age and pain, and she smiled with years of gravity pawing at her skin.

Pity brought Robin's eyes to the woman's wares, and her brows lifted at the stunning pieces of jewelry. "I need to get going, but your stuff is beautiful."

"Here. Hold on a moment. I have just the thing for you." The woman bent over, and Robin half expected to hear her spine crack.

"It's okay, really. I have to go."

The old woman rose and held out a necklace—a copper-colored chain holding an amethyst pendant. The stone shimmered a soft purple in the sunlight, a uniquely gorgeous piece, but with her job, jewelry wasn't practical. And when she wasn't at work? Jewelry was unnecessary. Where would she ever wear it?

"Five dollars and it's yours."

Seemed too good to be true.

With Robin's hesitation, the old woman added, "Amethyst has been known to grant your truest desire while protecting you from bad humors, so be careful how you use it." Her arm reached closer, urging her to accept the deal.

A gem would protect her? More like her nine-millimeter, which…she didn't bring. "Thank you, but no thanks."

"If you're in need of something you can't quite explain, you know where to go." The old lady returned the necklace under the table, but the smile never faltered.

With an awkward smile, Robin shimmied out of there, eyes glued to her phone. One last message, and she wouldn't feel guilty about abandoning the ship. She smiled at her silent pun. *I'm leaving, guys. Sorry I missed you.* She moved swiftly toward the hill where her car was parked.

The sounds of a man frantically panting pricked her ears. He shouted a word Robin didn't recognize. Her feet stopped. Something about it wasn't like Blenny playing games. It was real. Panic. Someone needed help. Robin tucked her phone into her purse, took the strap and slung it across her body to keep it out of her way, and turned, senses heightened for an emergency.

Her mouth dropped open at the shocking sight.

4

Chapter 4

Nassau, New Providence Island, Bahamas, 1715

RILEY COLLECTED HIS COCKED hat with the frilly feathers—the finest wear reserved only for shore leave—and meandered his way out onto the cobblestone street. He pushed his hat over his head to block out the blinding sun. Endless heat and humidity kept the sweat pouring under his layers of fine clothing: a long-tailed vest with carved buttons over a tunic, a lacy cravat, and a leather baldric currently sporting only a cutlass. The pistols were left on the ship to be cleaned, inventoried, and reloaded. The things misfired half the time and were terribly inaccurate the other half. Riley preferred swords and knives. His own skill was what he trusted when the time arose.

He headed down to the water where small waves shimmied the surface of the Caribbean Sea. A few sleepy boats rocked in the bay and sails dotted the horizon, but he recognized only a couple. A grove of palm trees shook with the breeze, and as Riley approached, sand entered his boots. Away from the noise of the town, the gulls kept him company.

Next to the water's edge, Riley sat on a homemade chair and leaned against an abandoned hut, resting in the shade, and used his hat to fan his face. He didn't know who crafted the small escape from town, but if they returned, he relinquish his seat.

The path to Fort James would send them through the *Peibo del ler San Francisco*'s territory, a hundred-gun, first-rate Spanish man-o'-war. A ship where both Price and Randall, among others, had been prisoners. The men understood the near-insurmountable risk ahead of them. And William Price was right to be concerned over the cliffs of the Gambia River. If Spain, indeed, found them, the crew's English schooner was no match for the warship. Taking the English castle was the most dangerous plan imaginable, but if these men would dash into a guarded hut for a chance at gold, they would raid a castle for the untold sums hidden below. Frankly, he'd expected more resistance for his plan.

A glimmer in the sand caught Riley's eye. It wasn't the green of an onion bottle, nor the silver of a blade, nor the gold of a piece of eight. Curious, Riley leaned over and lifted it free. In his palm rested a necklace...one he'd seen before. The chain, a copper metal, and the amulet, a striking violet. Where had he seen such a gem before?

Riley bounced it in his hand, shaking off the loose sand, trying but failing to pull the images from memory. Either way, it was valuable, and he wouldn't let it go.

"Riley! I thought it was you!" The familiar voice stiffened Riley's spine. A short man in a clean dress approached with a smile behind deadly eyes.

Riley closed his fingers over the amulet and checked the man's hands for a pistol or a blade, but he found none. Still, Riley didn't relax. Standing to his full height, he said with a friendly but stilted tone, "Vallo. What brings you here?"

"I've been searching for you."

Not long ago, Vallo had been in close ties with Captain Henry Price to fish their own crew for traitors. After performing his duty, Vallo turned on the captain and almost killed him. Vallo had been secretly in league with Spain and *Capitán* Delgado of the *Peibo del ler San Francisco* the whole time. And he was rewarded handsomely for his efforts with a share of the loot the crew had taken. No one had seen the traitor since. At present, none of the sails in the bay or on the horizon displayed the red crosses of Spain.

"I can't imagine why," Riley said, keeping his distance and watching Vallo's movements closely.

"The *Angelfish* out there, that's yours now?"

"It is."

During their escape from the Spanish warship and under a blinding and deafening full broadside, Riley assisted Price in commandeering the English schooner, Spain's prize. Since renamed the *Angelfish*, Riley never saw or heard of a connection between Vallo and the schooner.

"I lost something of mine, and I think it was left on the schooner. Did your crew find anything on board?"

Vallo's presence was bad news, and the sooner he rid himself of the traitor, the better. A mockery of an offer should be sufficient. "Nothing out of the ordinary, unless you had personal chickens."

Vallo's face twisted with confusion. "You only found chickens?"

"If you want, I can drop by the bank and request a fair sum in exchange." It was a bluff to keep the peace. Riley had no intention of paying Vallo anything after what the man had done to the crew.

"I'm not sure I understand."

Riley continued, this time giving truth, "According to Giles, only the chicken count was beyond ordinary. If it's not chickens you're missing, what is it?"

With a frown, Vallo turned away and gestured to dismiss him.

Riley didn't like that slight. "I insist. I want to make this right. Many things have happened between us, and I want no one to harbor ill will."

Vallo stopped and turned. "I prefer to see the hold for myself. I'll let you know if I find what I'm looking for."

He didn't want that man anywhere near their ship. "As captain of the *Angelfish*—"

"Worry not, I shall take care of the problem myself. The crew knows me well enough to grant permission to board," Vallo said with a smirk.

Randall's new recruits would have never met Vallo, and half the current crew was oblivious to Vallo's treachery to keep Henry Price from looking weak. Only a handful of men knew the full extent of the traitor's crimes, and they wouldn't be enough to convince the crew to forbid a seasoned sailor's presence. Not when the promise of a fort's hold required more sailors. And Vallo would be smart enough to show up with a fabricated story, rather than outright demanding his treasure back. The pittance remaining in the hold would only enrage him. Since Vallo wasn't the direct type, Riley worried what he'd do in retaliation.

Riley's hands balled into fists of frustration. The necklace he'd forgotten about cut into his palm. Rather than drop it on the sand, he lifted the familiar amulet over his head. "As the captain of the *Angelfish*," he repeated, "I order you to stay away."

The traitor turned back over his shoulder and smirked.

The necklace fell around Riley's neck, and with a blink, the sand underfoot disappeared. The humid salty air vanished. The temperature dropped. Most concerning, Vallo was gone.

But where did the sand go?

"Vallo!" Riley shouted, turning in place. "Vallo!" The grass under his sandy boots was unlike any he'd seen since...England. The ships at the dock were familiar, yet unrecognizable. The people around him wore...what exactly? Women wore breeches of a material he couldn't guess. Men wore shirts on the outsides of their outfits, and not one man wore a cocked...

Riley sighed in relief. One man, in point of fact, wore a cocked hat. As the man strolled by, it was of a material Riley hadn't seen. The necklaces draped around the man's neck jingled with a sound he'd never heard, and the bright red and black stripes of his breeches weren't familiar either.

Riley's heart pounded in his chest. He was too hot. He spun in place, breaths pulling in and out of his chest.

"Vallo!"

The cool breeze dried his sweat, sending chills along his skin, but yet, he burned up.

Where was Riley?

5

Chapter 5

Instincts taking over, Robin rushed through the meandering crowd and stopped short. Up close was so much worse. The distressed man smelled like he'd rolled out of a dumpster. His costume was old, tattered, and clearly handmade—a blue coat with gold buttons over a black vest and an ivory tunic, which altogether was way too warm for this weather. His breeches were brown, and his boots were black leather. A black tricorn hat with silly feathers covered his dark hair pulled into a ponytail tied with a ribbon. His wild eyes were dilated with confusion, and the look of horror—and a crooked lift of his lips on his bearded face broke her heart. Had he been drugged? And where is that smell coming from?

Either way, this man needed help now.

With hands held out to prevent defensive aggression, Robin approached cautiously. "Sir? Sir, are you all right?"

The man looked at her, but his gaze was unfocused, searching. What happened to this guy?

"It's going to be okay now. Take a deep breath." She declined to state her disclaimer. Since Robin was off duty, there was no need to incite further panic from those uneasy around law enforcement. The scent of liquor wafted off him, and Robin relaxed. Likely a case of spiked drink. "I'm Robin. What's your name?"

"Riley. Noah Riley." The man returned to scanning the area. His mouth gaped open, and his arms hovered around his waist as if on the verge of wanting to shoot, but he carried no gun. He was afraid, and Robin sensed he was lost. With Halloween months away, where else would a man dressed as a pirate go than the Tall Ships festival? Robin herself looked ridiculous as well, and she pushed that image down deep. She had a job to do.

"I'm Robin Hall. Do you know where you are?"

Riley met her gaze and took in her ridiculous outfit. Heat flashed behind his eyes. His dark features were certainly handsome, although hidden behind a beard, tangled hair that had fallen out of the ponytail, and sweat glistening on his high cheekbones. And the silly costume. Now was not the time. Robin focused on getting the man help.

"This was sand a moment ago." Riley shifted his weight and lost his balance, falling over onto the grass. A long sword angled awkwardly from his hip. Based on what she saw at the vendor, his was real. Riley was a true enthusiast. He touched the trimmed blades as if feeling grass for the first time. "Seems the ale was mixed too strongly today."

Robin smiled, assuming ale was some sort of mixed alcoholic drink. "I thought I smelled it on you. Do you need medical attention? I can call you an ambulance."

"You can what?" He looked up at her, puzzled.

"I can call you an ambulance," she repeated, louder and clearer. Riley only stared at her in confusion. Whatever he was on was strong. Robin reached for the man's wrist and waited for him to accept her help. "I'd like to check your pulse."

Riley hesitated before reaching his arm out to her. His eyes tracked to her exposed cleavage.

Robin wasn't surprised, but she kept herself professional. This man was clearly nothing like Blenny. She admired his high cheekbones and curving lips. His steely gray eyes were captivating, and she guessed he was in his mid-twenties—too young for her. But that shaggy long hair on his head pulled back into a pony was so rare to see and...alluring. Heat rose on her cheeks at her wandering thoughts, so unlike her.

Man in distress. Focus.

Robin slipped his coat up his wrist and heat rushed through her fingers. Actual heat. Was he running a fever? Robin felt for his pulse, but she wasn't wearing a watch. She dug out her phone, tapped the clock app, and started a time counter. Setting the phone down on the grass, she watched the digits change and focused on the hot skin beneath her fingers.

Eyes locked on her smartphone with a crack on the screen, his face turned ashen. "What is that?"

Robin laughed sarcastically. "I know it's old, but it still works. The department pays for my office-issue, and I don't see the need to have two newer phones."

"Department?"

Oh, shit. He was going to flip out. Better to rip off that bandage. "I'm a police officer, but I'm not going to hurt you. I need a minute to check your pulse and see if you're okay." She met his terrified gaze hidden beneath all those layers of grime. If he wasn't homeless, something bad must've happened to him. Pity tore through her.

"Where am I?" he asked.

"The Tall Ships festival." Robin looked over his clothes again, and the corner of her lips lifted. Chatting about his interest would help him relax. Robin could channel her inner Emily. "This is kind of cheesy, huh? I swear I don't dress like this on normal days. I was told this outfit would blend right in, and I guess you understand that. Did you make your costume? It looks so...authentic. And, uh, not at all cheesy." She didn't want to offend the guy as he was cooperating.

Riley glanced down at himself as if looking for the first time. In the short span of silence, Robin felt the pumping of his radial artery. The pulse was even but firing rapidly, which made sense considering his confusion and panic, but it didn't make sense considering his recent imbibing. Riley wasn't drunk.

"I think we need to get you to a hospital."

Riley pulled his arm away. "I don't need a hospital. Where am I?"

Perhaps his confusion went deeper than the festival grounds. Whoever drugged and dumped him here needed to be behind bars. "Look, you're in Wisconsin, and I promise I'll keep you safe."

He gazed into her eyes, completely baffled.

"I know it sounds weird, but you can trust me. You're in good hands." He didn't seem afraid of her job title, which was a relief, but after she'd lost her mom and caused Officer Clark Thompson's death, she didn't take her promises lightly. This guy was in trouble, and Emily would insist a fellow pirate enthusiast be kept safe, and that was what Robin intended to do.

"Where's that...Wisconsin?"

Robin noticed his English accent. It sounded almost....elite. Was he royalty or someone important in Parliament? Judging by his disheveled appearance, he likely couldn't handle an American medical bill, and by his complete confusion about being here, he probably didn't purchase a health plan for travelers. Robin was going to have to help in a different way.

"How about something to eat? Are you hungry?"

"Quite famished."

Robin rose to her feet and held out a hand to assist him up. She didn't want him to fall again; then she would have to send him to the hospital, regardless of the consequences.

Riley looked at her hand like it was poison.

"Take it. Let me help you. Trust me, you don't want to injure yourself on this side of the pond." Her hand hung in the air, waiting.

With a frown, Riley pulled himself to his feet, and Robin let her hand drop. She chalked that up to cultural differences, not a sexist slight.

"What are you in the mood for? The festival has burgers, hot dogs, brats, fries, and a few beer-battered deep-fried things—generally involving cheese—which are excellent by the way."

Riley's upper lip twitched like it all churned his stomach. Well, there weren't any vegan options here, unless fries counted.

"We'll keep it simple with burgers, but you have to try the cheese curds. It's mandatory for all Wisconsin visitors. This way." Robin headed straight toward the food tent, which at this hour had no line.

Riley stayed by her side, neck craning around like he'd never seen a portable kitchen before. How did a person travel half-way across the world and not remember it? Or deliberately put on those clothes for this festival and not remember his destination? The best she could offer was helping him remember where home was and safely putting him back on that plane—after she was certain he was sober from whatever caused the confusion. At this point, it had to be a drug-spiked drink. No vendors sold alcohol, so he didn't get it here, which only brought up more questions.

Robin placed their order and paid with a credit card. Riley watched her intently, but she wasn't concerned that he'd mug her. There was a genuine innocence there, not a manipulative con game. Even if he tried, she could take him. Collecting the plastic baskets of food, she handed one over to Riley.

He stared at it.

Robin chuckled. "You've seen hamburgers before, right?"

Riley stared at her, his eyes roaming her outfit once again, and heat rushed through her body as if his hands glided along her skin. If any other man looked at her like that, she'd give him a piece of her mind and a particular finger thrust in the air. It was the accent. Had to be. What American woman could resist the charms of an English accent? The allure of a different life, a different world. An escape.

Robin cleared her throat. "There's an open picnic table over there."

Riley followed her to a table and mimicked her sitting and pushing aside the tissue paper in the basket. She fisted her burger, elbows resting on the table, and took a big bite.

Rather than lift his own burger to dig in, Riley continued staring.

"I bought you lunch. The least you could do is try it. Here. Start with this." Robin pinched a deep-fried cheese curd and offered it to him.

He stared at it, face blank of expression.

"Come on. My hands are clean..." she trailed off at her insensitive gaffe. Nice move, Hall. *Go ahead and insult the homeless English guy.* She glanced aside.

Noah Riley took the juicy cheese curd from her fingers and reluctantly placed it into his mouth. He chewed slowly as if exploring the texture for the first time.

"How is it?"

"Different."

He spoke! But not enough. "Different good or different bad? What's the food like where you're from?"

"What is this?" Riley lifted a cheese curd out of the basket and inspected it.

"It's cheese with a coating."

"It's more pleasant than it looks, I admit." Riley placed the bite into his mouth, chewed, and swallowed. "On a bountiful day with fully stocked provisions, we feast on salted pork or chicken, potatoes, biscuit and rum. When provisions run low and rations are thin, we subsist on biscuit and diluted rum."

"That sounds bland." And dreadful. And clearly not the diet of a high-society man. Who was this Noah Riley?

"Food is only a means of survival. We hope to have sufficient quantities for the account, and that it won't spoil before we take shore leave." Riley lifted his burger and bit down. He chewed, gagged once, and swallowed. He wiped tears from his eyes. "That's...uh...bold of flavor."

"You're a sailor?"

The corner of his lips lifted. "Captain, newly minted, in fact."

Robin's brows rose. Even more interesting, his memory was returning. "Military or commercial?"

Riley smirked. "I declined to enlist in the Royal Navy after hearing of their decrepit conditions." He reluctantly took another bite and this time, he paused mid-chew, suppressing a gag. He was being polite.

"The Navy can't be that bad. Cramped, sure, but decrepit? That's a little harsh."

"I find my word choice is not wanting."

"What ship do you captain?" Robin asked, drawn to his story and trying to link where he'd come from to appearing in Wisconsin.

"After turning my back on the Royal Navy, I took up the black. I am one of the few who have no shame in it." He studied her face, waiting for a reaction.

She expected an answer similar to HMS *Queen Elizabeth*, or something generic like a submarine, or even I *cannot disclose that information.* "What's *the black*? Is that a commercial vessel?"

Riley cleared his throat and drank a few swallows with a grimace. Astonishment lifted his brows, and he asked, "You've never heard of the black?"

"Black what?"

Riley puffed out his chest in pride. "The black banner, of course. A crew of men, devoted to their cause, enemies to all mankind, and free of the Crown. Your lands have never experienced the marauders of the sea?"

Robin's rude snort broke through, and her lips pulled into a smile. "I should've known you're talking about pirates. I guess you're in the right place."

Lips pressed firmly, Riley wasn't amused. "In what world are pirates a laughing matter? Do we not instill fear in your people here?"

Was he delusional or a method actor? Since Robin enjoyed the conversation, and the man needed food to help sober him up, she humored him. "Pirates are fiction for children's tales. Not sure why? None of the true stories are child-friendly." At Riley's serious demeanor, she dropped the levity. "All right, fine. If you want a serious answer, there are pirates on the other side of the world. In small motorboats, they grab and smash before the authorities can catch them. But no, they aren't a concern here."

Having finished his meal, Riley downed the rest of his water and sat upright. "If you remain under British rule, then this is an oppressed world where freedoms are nothing but a veil."

"We aren't ruled by the British."

"Spain?" Riley asked.

Robin cocked a brow, and her phone chimed with a text. "Finally!" She dug out her phone and lit up the screen, but it wasn't Emily or Angela. Robin's enthusiasm sunk. An organization was begging for a blood donation. She followed Riley's gaze to the dock. The next ship had already unloaded and reloaded, heading back out. And another two more were closing the distance.

"What is that device? You said a phone. What is it?" Riley said, leaning forward.

This disheveled Englishman with an elite accent, who appeared and smelled homeless, claimed to be a captain, but not of a military or commercial vessel. A pirate captain, who didn't know what a phone was. This had to be beyond method acting, but if it wasn't, he was damned convincing. More realistically, this handsome man with his striking features and broad shoulders suffered from a poorly managed mental illness.

"It's a phone. You've heard of a phone, right?"

Riley didn't like her answer, and Robin could read anger when she saw it. Just like Blenny, it roared whenever he didn't get what he wanted. Next was demanding, then backpedaling and apologizing, like clockwork.

Instead, Riley shocked her.

6

Chapter 6

ROBIN HALL WAS BEYOND vexing. What madness had he been thrown into? More importantly, why was this strange woman so gracious to him? A woman officer. A woman who was stunningly beautiful with bright pink lips, bold hazel eyes, and brilliant red hair cascading in curls down her back and chest. A woman with an impossible palate. Everything she said was so confusing, and yet genuine. The phone device was in her hands. He couldn't deny its existence. The growing confusion only angered him, but his sharp tone was aimed at himself rather than her.

"I'm sorry to have burdened you with my lack of comprehension. Where I'm from there are no phones. Those sizzling machines under the tents don't exist, and not minutes ago, I was standing on the sandy beach of Nassau, but now I'm in Wisconsin—next to familiar yet different ships. I cannot explain what transpired, so pardon me, I'm simply frustrated."

Robin frowned and tucked that strange thing away. "You're serious?"

"As serious as a trip to the gibbet," Riley said flippantly.

Before she responded, he thought deeper on his remark. This woman wanted to help; that much was clear. Although facing the Crown and accepting just punishment was

Buckley's nightmare, Riley had only preferred to avoid it until the due time. One of two fates awaited all pirates. The preferred was death during the account and reuniting with all the crew he'd lost over the years—good men taken too soon. The alternative was death at the hands of the Crown, made into a public speckle on a gibbet.

After discovering Riley's mind had finally broken, there would be no honorable death a sea for him. Leaning forward in secrecy, he swallowed a lump caught in his throat. "You said you're an officer. Can you surrender me to the authorities?"

Robin rubbed her face and exhaled. "Yeah, you know what? This was fun and all, but I need to get you home. Authorities sounds good to me. What facility were you in? Summerset? Longview? Brown County?"

Riley didn't recognize any of those ships, but after the morning he had, he wasn't surprised. If he could find his ship, then he needn't succumb to the authorities at all, and he could save his crew from the danger they faced. He leaned forward in urgent secrecy. "*Angelfish*. I'm captain of the *Angelfish*. Have you heard of her?"

Robin twisted her lips and stood up. "Can't say that I have."

Riley glanced at the food and shifted his eyes to the strange objects surrounding him. Since he'd never heard of or seen these things before, they weren't trading with England. The goods never appeared on ships crossing the oceans. Robin and her unusual dress loomed over him. He'd seen it once before...on a strange woman...shortly before a squall sent the *Sea Lion* crashing against an outcrop off the coast of Cuba.

The stowaway who'd been lost and confused.

The magic woman Price had warned him about.

But this was wrong. Riley's hands trembled, and a sinking feeling crushed his chest. Impossible. All of this was impossible. It couldn't be, could it? Was traveling through time a regular occurrence here?

"What...what year is it?"

Robin chuckled. "Okay, now you need more help than I'm qualified for. You must've missed a dose of medication or something. We need to get you admitted, Captain Noah Riley. Is that your real name?" She held out her hand.

"What's the year?" he demanded harshly with a slam of his fist on the table. He needed to know the truth.

"I bought you lunch; you could be nicer."

Riley flinched. He had no right to take his frustrations out on her. She was only trying to help. "My apologies for scaring you. Please answer the question."

"What year do you think it is?" she asked carefully.

Riley rose to his full height, hand resting on the hilt of his cutlass. "Seventeen-fifteen."

Robin frowned. "Are you sure?"

Having lived on a ship packed with men since his teen years, Riley didn't have much experience with women, but he was certain her confusion was as genuine as his. The anger pumping through his veins softened, but his hands trembled harder.

"I captured an English schooner with my previous captain not weeks ago. We recovered a Spanish prize off the coast of Florida not months ago. I'm certain of the year."

"Well, I hate to break it to you, but you're off by about three hundred years. Let me call the station and see if there's an endangered missing person alert. Stay right here." Robin retrieved that phone from her coin purse again.

Three hundred years. Riley had fallen into...the future? His knees gave out, and Riley dropped onto the bench of the table. Robin rushed to his side, but seeing he was stable, she frowned and continued talking at the device.

Riley glanced at the tall ships docked, and his gaze tracked over the crowd in clothing both familiar and so foreign or scandalous he never would've imagined it. Robin was right. Riley was certainly missing...from his home centuries in the past.

He had no way of getting back, as he had no way of knowing how he'd gotten here. As soon as Robin handed him over to her authorities, his struggles would end, a fate he welcomed with open arms, because Riley would reunite with his family.

Riley missed his dear future-brother-in-law, and despite the circumstances, he missed his betrothed, too. Robin reminded him of her. Generous to a fault, blindly trusting, and admittedly stunning with lips that curved into shapes betraying her thoughts. It amused Riley to watch her mouth move against the phone. Her hazel eyes met his and shifted away. Again they came back, and...no, Robin was not like his betrothed. The young woman of his past was a burden he'd forever carry in his heart. Robin, though older than Riley, could never be a burden. She was simply...a bonny rescuer dropped into his path to guide his way off this mortal plane.

Robin tucked away her phone. "There's nothing the department is aware of. Let's get you down there and file a report. I've had enough of this place myself." She gestured for him to follow, and he stood on sea legs.

He'd sailed with the best men he'd ever known, and the worst scum with nary a flinch, knowing his end approached every day he sailed the seas. But facing down that reality was something else entirely. Robin watched Riley's unsteady knees, and she rushed to his side, supporting him, and holding his arm. But in his current state of confusion and resignation, he accepted the bonny rescuer.

"My car's this way."

Riley didn't know what that meant, but he allowed her to lead him up a small hill. His legs became stronger with each step, but people around them stared like they were animals. He deserved their scrutiny...and worse, but he carried no shame. He could not change the choices of his past, so he willfully accepted their disgust. If Robin knew all Riley's secrets, she'd join them in their prejudice.

Atop the hill, Riley froze in place. Bright shiny beasts lined up for the attack. One purred to life, and its eyes glowed in territorial fury. Riley had never seen such animals. His pulse raced, and instinctually, he pushed Robin behind him for her own safety. Unsheathing his cutlass he roared, "Back you beast! Back, or I shall slay you and dine on your entrails!"

Riley lifted his sword to strike, but he didn't know how the animal was going to attack—he'd never seen one before. Nevertheless, an end was still an end—via the Crown's gibbet or a beast. One was decidedly less drawn out and embarrassing. With a bellow, Riley charged, legs pumping full speed ahead. But after a step or two, he found himself knocked straight off his feet, and he landed on his back, immobile. His legs were weighed down. His arm pinned away. But how? The beast didn't move, and he never struck it. A magical beast from a magical world. "You haven't got the best of me yet! Unhand me and fight like the foul beast that you are!"

The weight pressing his chest was oddly warm. Peeling his furious glare from the beast, Riley glanced down, and to his surprise, Robin sprawled over his body, and her arms and legs tangled with his.

"Did you look that those models?" she scolded. "Do you have any idea the property damage you were facing? You can't do things like that here, understand?"

The beast had pinned her as well. Riley tried freeing her, but she wouldn't budge. "Are you injured, Lady Robin? Has the beast hurt you?"

Robin's lips twisted, and she shifted on his chest to meet him face to face. "Robin, just Robin. No lady. There is something wrong with you."

Impressed with her lack of fear, Riley said, "I feel no pain, and yet I cannot move. The magical beast has bested us both. I'm sorry I could not save you from it, and it's my fault for angering it. I beg of you to forgive me."

She only stared at him with disbelief.

"How bad is my injury?" he asked, still unable to move, hoping the end continues as swiftly and pain free.

"You're being serious," she said, gazing into his eyes. Worry framed her face. He didn't like that look.

Riley frowned. "I never laugh in the face of death. It's disrespectful."

"That's a car. I'm the one restraining you. If you calm down, I'll release you."

Riley shifted, trying to free himself, and indeed, feminine hands pinned him. How remarkable. Something else caught his eye entirely. As he shifted beneath her, friction developed against his body, and the most wonderful cleavage popped up to say hello. Heat rushed through Riley's body, pooling where he didn't want it. He looked at her chest again, helpless to look away.

"I saved you from a lawsuit." Robin sank back on her ankles, releasing him and taking the marvelous view with her. "What you say makes no sense at all, but a part of me wants to believe you. Let's get you cleaned up, and then I'll see what I can do, okay?" She offered her hand in assistance again, but being sturdy on his feet, he needed it not.

Riley rose on his own accord and followed her, reluctantly. He'd done many dangerous and wild things in his years, but never before had nerves affected him so. His legs were still loose but capable, his stomach gurgled, and the rapid fire of his heart made him feel like a young man alone with a woman for the first time. Nothing made sense to him, but he walked along in this strange world of the future, avoiding his sword nor his hand touching the shiny beasts, lest he stir them awake. The entire herd waited silently.

Bangs nearby turned his head, but Robin showed no concern.

Strange world indeed.

When Robin walked into another row of slumbering beasts, he couldn't do it. Riley's breaths became shallow. As she walked farther and farther from him, his chest squeezed. He tried focusing on her exposed backside as motivation to follow, but his body wouldn't move. One of the shiny beasts chirped and flashed nearby, and Riley startled in his skin.

Robin stopped and with a single bare hand, she peeled back the outer flesh of a beast, and it didn't protest. What sorcery was this?

"Sit right here. It won't hurt you."

She turned her head, and Riley still hadn't found his legs.

"Riley? It's okay. You have nothing to worry about." Robin returned to his side. With her hands gripping his arms, she pulled him toward the open flap of the beast.

He resisted, unable to coordinate his muscles, but somehow his legs moved, and Robin stopped him at the opening of the beast.

At one point, he'd stared down a Royal Navy man-o'-war opening its gunports on the verge of unleashing a full broadside without mercy. That had fueled Riley to spring into action. Another time, he'd stared down the barrel of a rifle during a standoff on shore. He'd hated to open fire on a fellow sailor, but the man left him no choice, and still, his hands and feet had reacted with expert timing. When the famed *Sea Lion* wrecked, Riley had gripped the mainmast. Because he'd never learned to swim, he watched in horror as he sank toward the abyss, but when the hull rested on the soft sand beneath and he remained above water, Riley leaped toward shore, knowing his own uncoordinated efforts were the difference between living and dying. Somehow, he'd made it to dry land, coughing and gasping, but he'd done it.

Riley stared at the shiny beast before him. Its flesh or wing hung open, daring him to climb inside, but he only stared. "You want me to what?"

"Sit on that seat." She pointed to a velvety shape, suspiciously shaped like a throne. "I'll close the door. It won't hurt you. I promise."

With shaky limbs, Riley folded, and Robin helped him lift his long legs inside the beast. His knees pressed against its firm insides, making his own stomach swirl with nausea. Robin shifted the seat, startling him, but leaving him more leg room.

"Watch your fingers. Here comes the door."

Riley gripped his thighs.

Robin closed the beast's wing and rushed around it, as if concerned for Riley's well-being. Riley only stared wide-eyed at all the gauges and buttons. Slipping into the seat abreast, she leaned over him, and Riley caught a whiff of her scent. Not of flowers or the salty sea, but a feminine fragrance of her own sweat. Quite pleasing.

A pleasant distraction.

Riley returned his eyes to the insides of the beast, and Robin's scent wasn't distracting enough. Finding a measure of comfort in her presence, his eyes followed her movements. "What are you doing?"

"Buckling in." Her arm brushed his chest, and Riley sucked in a breath. Heat rushed through his body and pooled in his lap. His palms squeezed his thighs harder.

A click startled him.

Robin sighed. "I'm going to move us now. If it's too much to bear, you can close your eyes. I won't judge."

She called him a coward. What nonsense! But since Riley's jaw clamped shut with tension, he couldn't dispute it.

Robin sent him a gentle smile, and her wrist twisted. The beast underneath roared with anger. Riley startled again and gasped. This was a mistake. He needed to get away from these monsters. He wasn't prepared to handle them. What weapons would work against such strong flesh? Not a cutlass, nor a dagger. He didn't believe a pistol capable either. A powder flask might do the job, of which he had none. His knuckles turned white, wishing for something to defend himself against these foreign creatures.

Robin pulled a lever, and the beast moved. "I know there's nothing I can say that will make this easier, but hang in there. You can do this."

Riley panted with his rapid heart rate.

"I should take you to the city campground to shower and then drop you off at the mental health crisis center. Not only would I not feel guilty about leaving you in the state you're in, but I would've fulfilled my sworn duty as an officer."

Robin didn't continue her statement, so Riley said, "I believe you had more to say."

A shy, feminine smile lifted her lovely lips. "I'm taking you to my place, where you can get real soap, hot water, and clean clothes. But I'm warning you, I know self-defense in case you've forgotten, and I'm good with weapons. If you try anything..." she trailed off, glancing at the shifted fabric in his lap.

Heat tore up his cheeks as he squeezed his thighs tighter. A forward woman. How novel. How distracting.

The beast left the area of the sleeping nest, and at once, many moved in a coordinated line. Riley sucked in a breath and released his painful grip on his thighs. Instead, he squeezed protrusions inside the beast. The cause of his discomfort would experience its own discomfort. Served it right. He didn't know what survival meant here, and every moment more of this world terrified him further.

At least it would end soon.

7

Chapter 7

Robin had dealt with mental illness cases before, but never anything like this. A mental patient with a foreign accent from the other side of the world on a spiked alcohol bender with a debilitating car phobia. Who also claimed to be a pirate captain from the year seventeen fifteen. None of this made sense. Public transportation was available, but Riley couldn't even handle *seeing* a car. The sooner she reached her Glock and spare mags and removed these hideous clothes, she'd feel safe and functional.

A quick clean up should help Riley sober. Once she got real answers, she could get him real help. Since no missing person report had been filed yet, perhaps a private nurse was about to clock in for her shift to find him gone. Or maybe the mental health facility hadn't done a head count on their padded rooms. Someone had to be looking for him.

Robin turned the wheel, guiding her car into her complex's parking lot while keeping the corner of her eye on this captain fellow with a wild imagination. She stopped the car in her assigned space, but Riley didn't move. Robin exited the vehicle, circled around, and opened the door for him. He still didn't move.

Riley's hands squeezed the arm rests, like a man terrified of flying who heard the notice for take-off.

"It's safe to come out now." She held out her hand.

Still nothing. Riley faced forward, body rigid with fear.

Robin leaned inside and unbuckled him. "Lift out your legs. It's okay. You can trust me."

He looked at her hand, and one leg at a time, he slowly climbed out of the car without taking it. She shut the door behind him, and he startled.

Robin shook her head and walked toward her brick two-story apartment building. Up the single step, she typed in the security code to the foyer. It beeped and flashed green, and Robin opened the door. There was no shadow of a man behind her. She turned.

Riley had moved away from the car, but he stared at the building. Now he was afraid of apartment complexes too? She didn't live in a dangerous area or anything. Letting the door close and relock, Robin scooped up Riley by the arm and dragged him to the door. He resisted, but only a little.

"This is your home?" he asked, perplexed.

Trying not to take offense to his confusion, her tone was clipped. "Second floor. Right this way." Robin pulled him through the main door, past the bank of mailboxes and the coin-op laundry machines, and up the stairs. At the rate he functioned, getting him cleaned and questioned would take all day.

Robin didn't have all day. She had applications to fill out so she could escape the hell that had become her job. Using a standard key, she unlocked her door and opened it. "This is me."

Robin walked in, never happier to be home, and she tossed her purse on the round kitchen table. She didn't hear the door close. Turning around, Robin found Riley standing at the threshold. "You're letting the air conditioning out."

Riley stared at her.

"You're not a vampire, are you?" she asked as a joke. "You can come in."

His eyes moved around her living room as if seeing a comfortable home for the first time. What kind of padded room did he stay in? The more time she spent with him, the more her pity grew and the less she wanted to return him to whatever those poor conditions must be.

With a patient sigh, Robin returned to the doorway and dragged the man inside and closed the door. "I have some menswear in my closet. Give me a minute to find it. It's been forever since anyone else's been in here."

Blenny had been right about that detail. She rarely brought men home, and never from her workplace. Along those same lines, she never had many visitors either. Well, none actually.

As Robin entered her bedroom, she averted her eyes from her mom's memorial on her end table. Heading straight to her small walk-in closet, she shuffled through stacks of folded clothes. Buried at the bottom was a pair of sweatpants and a plain T-shirt. She assessed the size and figured they'd fit well enough to get his outfit washed. She set the stack on her bedspread and returned to grab pants for herself. She peeked at Riley, who stood observing her home as before, and she closed the closet door. Robin changed her clothes, slipping into a comfortable T-shirt and tight jeans, excited to be free of the scratchy polyester. From the gun rack in her closet, she collected her Glock, checked the safety, and stuffed it into the back of her waistband until she was sure. Robin exhaled with a smile. Now she felt better.

Robin returned to the living room and dropped the folded stack onto the coffee table near Riley. She tracked his eyes to her beige carpet, empty white walls, and plain white appliances. It wasn't *that* interesting.

"It's so clean and spacious," he said in awe.

The evening sun made her apartment glow, casting long shadows across her floors, and her eyes strained. Robin flipped a light switch, and Riley looked up, lips parting slightly.

"Light in an instant? That's marvelous! What candles are these?"

Robin's turn to stare. Was he serious? Deadpan, she answered, "Bulbs. Not candles. Listen, the bathroom is right there. I have disposable razors in the top drawer and clean towels in the one below. Take a shower and clean up. I'll get your costume washed."

Riley looked down at himself. "I'm not wearing a costume."

Robin closed her eyes for a moment and gestured to him. "Your outfit. It needs washing."

Riley frowned. "A sprinkle of ale doesn't spoil my clothing."

Alcohol, nailed it. Robin chuckled. "I assure you; it needs to be washed."

Riley pressed his lips together and discreetly sniffed himself. With a nod, he went to the bathroom without the clean clothes. What was he planning on wearing instead? With a frown, Robin pulled out a jug of coffee grounds from an upper cabinet.

"Pardon me, ma'am," Riley said, leaning out of the bathroom. "Where do I find the water? The basin is fixed to its location."

Robin laughed. He was a master at keeping up this bizarre charade. Of all the things she could believe about this Captain Noah Riley, never having seen running water was not one of them. Robin pulled out two mugs and humored him. "Turn the knob, and I already told you to call me Robin."

Water gushed in the bathroom, and Riley laughed with the giddy joy of a child.

Robin shook her head with an infectious smile as she made them fresh coffee. His clothing landed on the floor with a heavy thump, and he closed the bathroom door. Robin retrieved his things.

He believed—what had he said?—the year was 1715. Well, he'd studied the period well. Robin lifted what amounted to rags to her. The stitching on his vest was something only Emily would admire. The breeches were tie-closed. No elastic. She was convinced every detail, down to his authentic cutlass, was meticulously period accurate.

Robin needed to introduce those two.

The bathroom door cracked open. "My apologies for my crude disposal of my clothes, but you insisted on their needing washing."

"Don't worry about it," Robin said from the living room.

If he were institutionalized his entire life, was it believable he'd never heard of cheese curds? Sure. But what institution would allow him an authentic sword? Riley must not be an escaped mental patient. So then what? His innocent interest in electricity and pure joy from running water seemed a little too authentic. Robin hadn't traveled to England ever, but were there villages without running water or cars, like an Amish society across the pond? She really had no idea. It was plausible, and more likely.

But then how did he get on a plane and not remember? Or get to the airport with a fear of cars?

Robin unsheathed part of his sword. It was dinged and scratched with use. Unbelievably real. Riley didn't need this here, as she didn't need her gun. Robin settled his things, removed her gun, and placed it into her purse. Just in case, she collected a few more mags from her gun closet and paused as a sweet melody came from the bathroom. The man sang beautifully. She smiled, hugging her mags.

What if he was from the past?

A glance at her mom's memorial had her sitting on the bedspread. "It's ridiculous, isn't it?" she asked her mom, but the photograph never responded. Sometimes she heard her mom's voice in her head, but as the years had gone by, her voice faded, almost like a punishment for failing to protect her. Robin missed her dearly. Her murder incessantly grated at her like a woodpecker's beak against a tree. Resolved. Determined. Unrelenting. Robin didn't know how to make it up to her, so she talked to her as if it never happened. "It almost makes sense. Do you think he's the captain of a pirate ship from 1715?"

Her mom's flowing waves and bright youthful smile never moved. She was laughing in this photo, taken by Robin's grandmother ten years before her mom's murder. Robin smiled back, wishing beyond everything she could've prevented that tragedy.

"I know, it is ridiculous. But what if the government discovered a method of time travel, and they kept it a secret? Considering they only admitted to having alien contact seventy years after the fact, it's plausible, isn't it?"

After giving her mom a chance to answer, which never came, Robin set the photo down with a sigh and returned to Riley's clothing. She sorted the washable from the non-washable. The leather looked hand-tanned and rough cut. Then dyed black, but the color wasn't perfectly even. This wasn't bought in a store.

The notes from his song, which she didn't recognize, lifted to a crescendo, and the water stopped.

What would it be like to travel through time? Scary, for one, especially going to the future. But going to the past and seeing what the history books described—probably a little fun. Maybe a lot fun if one could return home.

Like a vacation, of sorts. A temporary escape.

The door to the bathroom opened, billowing steam into her apartment, and breaking her wild thoughts.

"Pardon me, Miss Robin, but I seem to have forgotten the clothing you offered." Riley stepped out of the bathroom, holding a white fluffy towel around his waist. Loose wet hair and a pendant clung to his sculpted broad chest. Rounded muscles flickered with his small movements. Riley's clean-shaven face revealed bright teeth against sun-tanned skin, high cheekbones—she'd admired those before but were worth mentioning—and deep-set gray eyes. He smiled bashfully. He was simply gorgeous. Who knew something so beautiful could be hidden behind so many layers of grime and hair and...silly costume?

Robin exhaled. Twice.

Her face burned, and she collected the stack of clean clothing from the coffee table and brought it to him. Such a shame. She liked him better without clothes. Robin cleared her throat and cast her eyes aside, hiding her dopey smile behind her hand.

"Thank you, Miss Robin. What is that smell?"

"Coffee. That's, uh, coffee," Robin sputtered. Riley was incredibly attractive, and she needed to keep her head straight. He was in a vulnerable position, and that didn't give her free rein to lose herself. Speaking of reign, Robin needed to shake herself out of this unfamiliar and uncomfortable charge surging through her. "Who's the queen back home?"

"Queen?" Riley set the stack on the edge of the bathroom vanity, and yep, Robin still watched. His back muscles danced with his gentle movements. The vanity itself, after the man had shaved, was clean. Robin repeated her thought: *The man cleaned up after himself.* She was going to faint if she didn't sit.

Resting his hands against his hips, holding the towel in place, Riley said, "King George took up the throne last year, the Protestant bastard. But since I've renounced my loyalty to the Crown, they can have him."

He sounded so sure of his words. For the first time since she'd met him, he wasn't confused. Inferring from his statement, Robin asked, "You're Catholic?"

Riley made a dismissive noise. "Absolutely not, but the king isn't of royal blood. Strategic positioning rained good fortune upon him, handing him England, Ireland, and the Electorate of Hanover."

Curious about this strong opinion and incredible detail, she asked, "So you prefer only pureblood royals take the succession?"

"He manipulates people, winning himself vast wealth and the support of half a country. At the same time, everyone else is only trying to earn a living, and what do we get for it? Branded a traitor and threats of the noose. Then the newspapers deliver *eyewitness* accounts, who've never been on a ship in their lives, but the readers take their word as gospel. What makes *him* different from us? Why do the people accept his actions but not ours?"

He lost her again. "You're the captain of a pirate ship. Doesn't that mean you avoid all the politics? I don't follow your anger."

Riley glared at her for a second, as if unwinding the fury within. Whatever this issue was, he felt strongly over it. His features softened, and his eyes followed her snug clothing. Robin stared at his most pleasant shape, likely thinking the same thing he was. Having a naked man in her apartment was a bad idea.

8

Chapter 8

RILEY SHOULDN'T HAVE UNLOADED his restrained energy on her—it was very inappropriate, but so were her distracting clothes. The woman wore pants! The tight curves were scandalous and highly revealing, but he couldn't look away. Of all the unbelievable things he'd seen today, one thing was certain: Robin Hall was a stunning woman. And any woman who could pin him on the ground so effortlessly and disarm him, was fascinating...and distracting. He needed to change this dangerous course.

"When I was in the washroom, I heard you speaking to someone. Did I miss them?" Riley craned his neck around, seeking the hidden visitor. Dressed in only a damp towel, he was in no condition to meet anyone, but he needed an excuse to break this unspoken lust surging through him.

Robin blinked. "I was talking to myself."

Riley's brows lifted.

"Um, well, my mom," she corrected.

"Might I meet her?" Riley had some questions of his own, like how a woman became an officer and learned to overpower him. And how did she command the shiny beast? Such feats were beyond his comprehension. Her mom must be an amazing woman as well.

Robin's spirits visibly fell. He'd hurt her, but he didn't know why. She shook her head and disappeared into her bedroom. Holding the towel at his waist, he followed her, unwilling to allow his blunder to be brushed aside. She dropped onto the bouncy bed and lifted a frame from an end table. After a wistful smile crossed her lips, she turned its face for him to see.

Riley sat next to her. With the towel secured under and around him, he accepted the frame, but his brows knitted in horror. This was no painting. He tipped the frame around. "Is your mother trapped in this? How did she get in here?" The colorful image of the smiling woman baffled him. What was this witchcraft?

Robin took the frame from his frantic hands, and her brow furrowed. "It's a photo. She's not..." Robin scrutinized him with a keen eye.

Riley only watched. He was truly horrified by this tiny woman.

Robin pressed her palm to her forehead as if fending off a headache. "Your sincerity is admirable. I'm so confused."

As was he. "How do you talk to her in there?"

Robin rubbed her thumb on the corner of the frame. "When I was a teenager, my mom was busy in the kitchen while I completed my homework in the living room. As a man in a ski mask rushed through the front door, my mom came around yelling at me, because she thought I was letting in a friend. She wasn't angry; her hearing had declined severely, so we yelled back and forth. My mom wanted to make them tea." Robin chuckled softly and sniffled.

Riley's hand rested on her thigh. Robin stared at it, but he didn't remove it.

Allowing his touch, she continued, "When I yelled back that it wasn't a friend, my mom saw him and stopped short. She told me to get the gun. Since it was the two of us, we keep—kept—a handgun in the house at all times for situations like this. Never used it before, but I ran, grabbed the thing, and aimed from around the corner of the kitchen. And when she repeated her urgent cry, I had the burglar in my sights, but I couldn't do it. I couldn't pull that trigger. What if I hit him, and it only made him angrier? What if I missed? What if...? The burglar grumbled about the yelling, and he shot her."

Riley only understood the important parts. "I'm so sorry."

Robin gripped the frame in her hands and anger curved her lips. "It's my fault she's dead. Only because he didn't see me, I was spared. He tossed the living room and the bathroom and took off with some pills and cash. I hid until he left and called for an ambulance. I held my mom's hands, and I selfishly begged her to stay with me. I apologized for not stopping the burglar. I told her it was all my fault, but only a bead of blood dribbled from her mouth. The wet sounds coming from her..." Emotion clogged her throat, and she swallowed thickly, as if trying to hide the painful memories. Robin inhaled deeply and blinked away tears. "When she'd bought the gun, we both promised to keep each other safe with it, but I failed. I failed her, and now she's dead."

Riley continued to hold her thigh. If she needed more reassurance, he'd give it, but he didn't want to force anything she wasn't comfortable with.

"I became a police officer because I wanted to stop men like him. I wanted to protect the innocent. But I couldn't even do that."

"Your mother's death wasn't your fault. It was the burglar's," Riley reasoned.

"You weren't there." Robin closed down and returned the frame to the table.

Riley rubbed her thigh and sent her a crooked smile. "You protected me from those shiny beasts, which I'm surprised you did, considering I was the instigator trampling on their territory."

A wet chuckle greeted his light comment. "Shiny beasts," she repeated quietly. "They're cars. Why don't you call them cars?"

Another reminder that Riley didn't belong here. Wearing nothing but a towel draped over his lap, and Robin being caught in a vulnerable moment was a dangerous combination. He'd made many mistakes in his past, and he wasn't going to add another to his long list—not right before judgment by the authorities. "If you'll pardon me, I shall dress now."

As he rose, her yearning eyes trailed along his damp chest and stopped at the amulet he'd picked up on the beach. Her interested face tilted as she scrutinized it.

She sniffled, clearing away her story, and rose. "That looks familiar. Where did you get it?" Without her boots, Robin stood a few inches shorter than his five-ten height, and she dragged a finger along the chain hanging from his neck. Heat followed her touch like a burning torch. Riley closed his eyes to fight off the desire pumping through his body and shifting the towel.

Where did he get it? Focus. He needed to focus on the piece of jewelry, not her soft fingers dancing along his skin.

Focus! Necklace. Sand. Sweltering heat and blistering sun. Images of what happened before he arrived in this confusing place returned to his mind like moving pictures. His heart rate sped up, and his breathing quickened. Eyes pulling wide, Riley exclaimed, "Vallo!"

He grasped the amulet with both hands, dropping the towel.

Robin sucked in a breath and turned around, shielding her eyes. "I'm sorry! I didn't know *Vallo* meant you were going to get naked. Next time warn me with something more obvious."

Riley picked up the towel haphazardly, holding in front of himself one-handed. "I must return to my crew before Vallo destroys them."

"Whoa, slow down." Robin pinched the bridge of her nose and caught a glance at him to be sure he was covered. He liked that his appearance flustered her, but now was the worst time. "If—and I mean a big 'if' here, because I'm not crazy, but *if* you are from the past, how did you get here?"

After commandeering the English schooner, renamed the *Angelfish*, he'd had a conversation with his previous captain, Henry Price, who'd explained the unbelievable tale. Riley lifted the amulet over his head and held it out on his open palm, displaying the gem under the blindingly bright unexplainable indoor lights. "With this. I found it on the beach."

"I think I've seen that before." Robin tilted her face at it, studying its color.

"I thought it familiar as well, which is why I picked it up."

"How does it work?" Robin touched the gem, tilting it, and it reflected off the overhead lights. "You know, assuming this is real."

Riley exhaled. He hadn't thought about it before but remembering his experiences with women appearing on the crew and staying in the past, a sinking sensation in his gut pulled his excitement down. On a deep sigh, Riley said, "I know not, but from what I've seen, the necklace only works one way."

His crew was blind to the danger before them. Without Riley, they had to discover Vallo's past before the traitor got them all killed. And if they survived and intended to take Fort James on their own, they had to elect a new captain to lead them. Everything he knew was over.

Everything he was—his name, his accomplishments, his trustworthy friends—it was all over, caught in a land of shiny beasts and automatic lights. Facing this fascinating woman before him, six-and-twenty years was too short, but Riley didn't get to choose that. With an air of defeat, Riley said, "I think it's best if you deliver me to the authorities."

Robin squinted at him before her face relaxed. She stared at his magic necklace. "Oh, the police station? I... I don't know if they can help you."

Defeated once again, Riley dropped the necklace onto his hat and collected his personal effects. His sword slipped a few inches free of its sheath.

"Can I see it?" Robin asked with a spark of interest in her eye. "It seemed so authentic. I'm not a swordsmith myself, but I was impressed."

The sword was useless against the beasts of this world. Head hung low, he handed over his cutlass.

"It looks so real," she said, sliding a finger along the imperfect edge.

Sharpness permeated his tone. "Of course it's real. What else would it be?"

"A prop." Robin gave him a curious look and said, "Did you get it from the vendor at the festival? But it looks heavily used. Do you train with it?"

Riley tilted his chin up. "I keep my sword in serviceable condition, as required by the articles. It's both capable of severing a line on deck or slaying an enemy." At least, an enemy made of flesh.

"Okay, okay. I didn't mean to offend you. Look, you being here might feel strange and scary, but I'm as confused as you are. I know people really get into the reenactment stuff, but the only pirate swords I've seen before today were plastic."

"You said there were no pirates." In that case, he needed to keep his sword. He could only imagine how much more ruthless these pirates were. Riley held out his hands to take it back from her.

"Pretend. Costume. Halloween, you know? My outfit was pretend, too."

Riley's lips parted, and he took his sword back with a frown and hastily shoved it back into his bandolier. "You people *pretend* to be pirates? What insanity is this?"

Robin's hand rested on his forearm. "It's not insane to pretend. It is insane to believe."

"Pardon me, ma'am," Riley said coldly and returned to the washroom. He closed the door and stared at his unfamiliar face in the mirror. He had lost himself in more ways than he imagined.

"I'm going to wash your clothes. I'll be right back," Robin called through the door, and Riley stared at it, unwilling to answer her.

A different door closed, leaving him in silence.

With nothing better to do, Riley dressed in the outfit stacked on the vanity. Comfortable, stretchy, but a little snug in places. He raked a hand through his damp hair and pulled it back. Finding his ribbon on the floor, he tied his hair at the nape of his neck. He smelled like a bowl of fruit, but he looked clean for the first time in ages. That was one thing he could get used to.

Being treated like an imbecile was not.

Left alone with a deep curiosity, Riley browsed her living quarters. The strange 'photo' of Robin with her mom showed them both warm and radiating love—something missing in Robin now. A persistent sadness settled beneath the surface—easy to see when he knew it well.

Next to the photo was a small ceramic pot with a floral design painted with expert precision—a level Riley hadn't seen before. He lifted the lid and frowned. Ashes? Why would Robin keep ashes? He replaced the lid and lifted a locket next to it. His thick fingers fumbled with the clasp, but he opened it. Robin as a child and the same smiling mom.

No father.

No siblings.

There were no other photos in the room.

Was she as lonely as he?

Chapter 9

Robin pushed Riley's clothes into the wash machine downstairs. She dropped in the coins and switched the knob over to the shortest delicate cycle. She'd hate to destroy his costume. The way he dressed meant he cared for it deeply, reminding her of Emily's enthusiasm for pirate history.

Everything he told her seemed like the ramblings of a delusional man, like he believed he was a real pirate. She wasn't enough of a historian to know if the facts checked out about King George, but considering his level of detail and passionate opinions, he'd likely memorized every historical text to back up his stories. Another clear sign of mental illness.

Or at least an unhealthy level of obsession, and Emily still functioned. And now this mentally ill patient was currently alone in her apartment. What made her trust him when she wouldn't allow her own colleagues inside?

When Riley had stepped out of the bathroom, dripping wet with a towel around his waist, showing off sculpted angles and sexy hair reaching a little beyond his collarbones, Robin hadn't wanted anyone more than him. And when the towel dropped, she had to hold herself back from his semi-erect state. She hadn't been that attracted to someone ever.

But he seemed mentally ill. Except his belongings wouldn't be allowed inside a facility. If someone stored his things for him, Riley would've gone back to that person. His sculpted physique wasn't possible while confined to a padded room. His passionate ramblings were coherent and reasonable—things she never saw in drug cases or mental patients. He absolutely didn't know what a car was, and his accent was as authentic as she could tell...as was his sword.

All signs pointed to him telling the truth.

But it wasn't possible.

So, Robin circled back around. She needed a straight answer out of him, so she could get him back where he belonged.

It was getting late, and Riley couldn't stay the night—not with him being so tempting. And she needed to check in with her friends. Robin was going owe Emily and Angela a girls' night out for bailing on them. Robin lifted her phone and checked the screen. Still no messages.

Weird.

When short gentle cycle finished, she lifted the outfit. The time spent handcrafting the clothing was impressive. He didn't use a machine. The stitches were uneven, handcrafted. Riley put love into crafting his outfit, so she wouldn't put it in the dryer. Plus, leather.

As depressing as reality could be, Riley, like her, had to face the real world.

RILEY KNEW WHAT LONELINESS felt like. He had his crew, many dedicated completely to him, but those sea dogs were no substitute for a family. With a fresh sadness weighing him down, Riley closed the locket and went to the kitchen to find a meal. He opened cabinets and found nothing familiar besides pots and pans. Even if he knew how to cook, he had no idea how to start a fire here.

Trusting that Robin wouldn't leave him alone with dangerous creatures, Riley pulled the handle on the large white thing. Cold air blasted him in the face. What a marvel! He recognized nothing inside, but he knew it was supposed to be food. Cooled food! Right inside the kitchen!

The front door opened, catching Riley in the act. He was giddy with his discovery. "I don't know what any of this is. How does it stay cold? It's amazing!"

He shut the wondrous creation, and Robin held his clothing hanging over her arm. "I didn't want to put leather in the dryer. It's still damp from the spin cycle, but it shouldn't take long to dry." She draped the clothing over the backrest of a chair. "Find anything good to eat?" That air of sadness still hung in her voice.

"Thank you kindly, ma'am."

"Robin," she said on a breath. "Just Robin. Look, it's getting late. I have a lot of work to do tomorrow that can't wait." She gestured to a sleek silver rectangle on the table, but Riley had no idea what that meant. "Can you tell me your name?

Where you came from? As much fun as this has been, I need to return to real life. You should too."

What was this accusation? Anger furled in his stomach. "I've been truthful with you."

Robin sighed. "Well, if that's the position you insist on, you can't stay here. Get dressed in your own clothes, and I'll bring you to the station."

His anger melded into a rock, settling heavily on his chest. He'd known this end would come, but for the flicker of a few hours, he'd enjoyed himself for the first time in a long while. He hoped to explore the spark between him and Robin. Instead, he cast his gaze aside. "Understood."

"I need a shower. Feel free to use the living room here to change. I won't spy on you."

Riley turned his back on her and waited until she turned on the water in the bathroom. He dressed in his breeches, tunic, and leather vest. He strapped his bandolier belt around his waist and over his shoulder. He holstered the cutlass and stepped into his boots. Finally he shrugged into his coat. Although, the coat was a little warm, shore leave or not, but sometimes appearances caused discomfort. He pushed his cocked hat onto his head and the tinkle of metal remaining on the table turned his head. The amulet. Seeing as he had nothing left of value, maybe the authorities would think better of him decorated with an expensive gem. He set his hat down and collected the amulet.

Riley slipped the amulet back over his head.

Chapter 10

ROBIN HAD BROUGHT HER own clean clothes into the bathroom so Riley could change in private. She chose clean skinny jeans and a T-shirt to take Captain Noah Riley and his crazy story down to the station. Maybe when he saw how serious she was, he'd come clean with the truth, and she could simply change directions in the car. Robin squeezed her wet hair with a clean towel and opened the bathroom door. "Coming out. Let me know if you aren't ready."

He didn't respond.

Robin frowned and leaned around the door. "Riley?"

Still nothing. Where was he?

Robin crossed to her bedroom and peeked inside. Not there. She returned to the living room, nope, and swung around to the fridge. Her apartment wasn't that big. She moved to the patio and stepped outside, scanning the area for a man in a pirate costume on foot. In the dusk, she found no one matching his description.

"Riley!" she shouted. A resident in the parking lot looked at her like she was nuts. Her face heated, and Robin went back inside.

Where did he go so fast?

Robin turned around and found the borrowed clothing folded neatly. His costume was gone, but he'd left behind his frilly tricorne hat. Why would he leave it behind? Was he trying to tell her something? Did he remember where home was and left? Did he change his mind about going to the police station? So many questions and no answers.

Robin checked inside her purse, in case this ruse was an elaborate theft, but her Glock, spare mags, and wallet were intact. She stared at the hat of a man, so wild in his choices and passions, and a small smile lifted her lips. "You do whatever you want, whenever you want, and no one can force you to do anything you don't want to. I can admire that."

Her eyes returned to her patio doors, and the smile slid away. He had to be out there, now even more lost and confused. Scared. She'd promised herself she'd keep him safe, and the way he reacted to cars would mean he'd react dangerously to traffic. She could flick on the scanner and wait for the inevitable call about a man in a costume attacking cars with a sword.

If he didn't get hit first.

Robin grabbed her purse and jumped in her car. She closed the door behind her and stopped. "This is crazy. What am I doing? I'm going to go chasing after an ill man who ran away from me?" She gripped the steering wheel and gazed beyond the parking lot. But if she didn't go…

"I can't leave him all alone, lost in the throes of panic. I'll make a few passes around a couple blocks, up and down. He couldn't have gone far. I can do that, yeah. It's not crazy; it's my duty—the duty to safeguard lives and protect the innocent. Then at least I tried. Right? Tell me I'm not crazy."

There was nothing in her car capable of answering.

Robin groaned and started the engine. She turned on her headlights and pulled out of the parking lot. With the festival wrapping up for the evening on the other side of the city, traffic was light. She rolled down the roads as slow as she could get away with while searching for any and all pedestrians. More specifically, for a handsome face with a stunning body—miles of muscles, carved to perfection, slick with steam.

Robin couldn't have imagined a man's form more pleasing to the eye than Captain Noah Riley, whoever he was. Heat rushed up her face—both in the raging desire for him but also in shame. Riley was a vulnerable man, and she had no right to think of him that way.

But she could still be a respectable person who completed her job with dignity and ethics while still daydreaming about his perfectly sized, partially raised mast between his legs? Robin turned on the car's radio, needing a distraction.

At the corner of her next turn, a few people waited for the city bus, wearing jeans and T-shirts or shorts and hoodies. Still, she kept going while checking the clock on her dash. This was crazy, wasn't it? Driving around near-dark looking for a harmless innocent man who'd walked away from her, a man she didn't know, a man who, by all accounts, was mentally ill.

With a sigh, Robin turned around and went home. She changed into lightweight pajamas, and after a nice cup of hot cocoa, she distracted herself with television, but her eyes fell on Riley's tricorne hat every few minutes. And after darkness fell, she no longer glanced out her patio door.

Instead, she turned down the volume on the television in case Riley shouted for her attention.

He didn't.

ROBIN BLINKED AS THE numbers on the alarm clock switched over. With a groan, she turned it off before it buzzed. How many cups of coffee would she need to get by with no sleep? Robin rolled out of bed and shuffled to the coffee pot, which was programmed to have a cup ready for her. Good ol' trusty coffee pot.

Robin poured a mug and turned around. He was real, wasn't he? She didn't dream she brought a complete stranger into her apartment, did she? Leaning against the counter, the tricorne hat stared at her.

Robin crossed to her patio and stepped out for fresh air. Crisp morning dew clung to her bare arms. Birds flew from maple tree to pine tree, singing and chirping. The sunrise bathed the landscape in pinks and purples, lighting the parking lot and front door of her complex. Maybe he came back and slept outside her door, uncertain how to buzz her apartment.

Riley was not there.

Robin sipped her coffee and went to her bedroom. On the end table, she rested her steaming mug next to Mom's smiling face. Riley had said her failure to pull the trigger wasn't her fault, and her mom's death wasn't her fault. "He was wrong; you know that."

Mom smiled.

She knew.

Robin dressed in the same T-shirt and skinny jeans from yesterday, because they weren't worn long enough to justify another round in the coin-op downstairs. Retrieving her mug, the gleaming laptop called to her. Robin sat at the table. Remembering Riley's bold assertions and strong passions—no matter how strange, Riley did what he wanted, when he wanted, and he wouldn't be forced to do anything he didn't want to—including taking off to avoid returning to his facility. He was free, and despite appearing lost, he was happy. Taking a page from his book, Robin refused to work with a bunch of men who'd created a hostile work environment. And right now, she wanted to end that chapter of her life.

With a smile on her face, Robin opened her laptop, chugged the rest of her cooled coffee, and typed up a resignation letter. After it printed, she signed it and smiled. This was her freedom. This was her saying no more, that she was in control of her life. To be honest with herself, two days ago she wouldn't have made this move. Likely, Robin would've typed it up, signed it, and tossed it. She had bills to pay, and no job lined up. It was irresponsible. It was rash. It was everything Robin wasn't. Instead, Robin grabbed her purse and keys, and Riley's fancy hat.

Pushing through the police department doors on a quiet Sunday morning, Robin's stomach twisted in knots. She could do this, no big deal. The corners of her eyes searched for judging eyeballs, but the office was thin. No one paid her attention. She strolled toward the officer in charge, hunched over a desk, and she stopped short. "Blenny? I thought you had the weekend off?"

The towering detective in a suit turned around and smiled. He leaned his bulk against the desk and folded his arms over his broad chest. "Riggs needed the day off, surprise family function. What can I do for you?"

"You can take this to the lieutenant when he comes in." Robin handed him her resignation letter folded in an unsealed envelope. "And these." She dug her badge and office-issue cell phone out of her purse and held them out to him.

Blenny's face was surprisingly disappointed as he collected the phone and badge from her hands. "You can't leave. You've only been here a couple months. Is it something I said? 'Cause you know I was joking, right?"

"Blenny. It wasn't what you said." *It was Riley.* Robin smiled. "Bye."

Robin turned on her heels and left while Blenny's mouth hung open, catching flies.

IN HER CAR, SHE checked her phone for messages from Emily or Angela, but she had none. That was worrisome. Maybe their phones fell overboard or somehow got damaged by water. Or they were too drunk and having too much fun to respond. That was more likely.

But to be safe, Robin pulled out of the department parking lot and crossed town to the festival. She motored up and down the rows and stopped at Angela's car. With her lips pressed thin, she pulled in alongside it. "Figures."

Taking Riley's hat with her, Robin got out of her car and cupped her hands around her eyes. She peered into Angela's driver side window. Empty.

Robin slung her purse over her shoulders, across body, and double checked her Glock and spare mags. She was no longer an active officer, but that wasn't going to stop her from coming to anyone's assistance. Robin walked to the festival grounds, scanning for familiar faces.

Who was she really looking for? Brushing that thought aside, Robin took in the sights. The tall ships slumbered dockside. The tents were erected but quiet. A few vendors were setting up for the day and the scent of cooking oil wafted over. A couple people were sleeping on picnic tables. Robin walked by each person, checking for her friends, but they weren't here.

Neither was Riley.

He'd left his hat as a message, she was sure of it, like he'd called to her to find him. But he would've come here. This was his home in a way, his comfort zone. Where was he?

Unless he gave up waiting.

Robin refused to believe that. She stroked the velvety trim.

Unless he remembered who he really was and went home.

No, he'd been far too adamant that he wasn't crazy. There was no way he'd voluntarily return to whatever home had suppressed him.

She kept moving, kept searching. Strolling by the vendor tables, a gravelly voice called to her, "If you're in need of something you can't quite explain, you returned to the right place."

It was the old woman, the seller of beautiful necklaces. Wait a minute. A delicious image came to mind: Wet Riley, naked, holding a towel precariously placed. A shiny amethyst pendant on a copper chain hung from his neck. Now she remembered why the necklace was familiar.

Robin stopped and smiled. "I *am* looking for something. You remember me, right? I was here yesterday, and you offered me a necklace for five dollars. Do you still have it?"

Or had Riley bought it?

The old woman's smile lifted her wrinkles. She bent at the waist and fished under the table while Robin scanned the people filtering in for the day. The old woman straightened, and her slender arm held the gem out to her. It glistened in the morning light, simply stunning. "It's yours."

Robin dug in her purse, unzipped her wallet, and flash a Lincoln.

The woman held out a palm to reject Robin's payment. "Don't worry about it. What am I going to do with it?"

Robin frowned. What kind of person didn't want money?

The old woman's thin arm bounced, insisting Robin take the necklace free of charge.

Robin checked the ground beside the woman's feet for a cash box. Why would she offer Robin a free necklace? There was no way the woman could've known Robin quit her job this morning. "I can't take it for nothing. Please, I insist." Robin held out the bill while accepting the necklace.

The stubborn and confusing woman wouldn't take it. Holding her hands clasped loosely in front of her, she nodded and smiled. "Good luck and safe journey."

Robin didn't know what to think. Such a strange thing to say, like a salute to someone leaving on a momentous occasion. Was Robin quitting her job that obvious on her face? With creepy suspicion, Robin set the bill on the woman's table anyway and nodded her thanks.

Walking away, Robin marveled at the gem, glinting off the morning's warm sun. It was the same one Riley wore, but he said he found his on a beach back home. He must've been delusional. She had no other explanation, but either way, Robin needed to get him out of her head. Just because she promised to keep him safe, didn't bind her to it forever. As much as the gesture held meaning, adults broke promises. Riley had left on his own accord, and she didn't own him.

Robin walked back to the parking lot, ready to fill out some job applications, because that was what responsible adults did after quitting on a whim. She frowned at Riley's hat. He would've wanted it back.

Robin placed her reminder of Riley over her head.

Chapter 11

IN THE BLINK OF an eye, Noah Riley stood on the beach in Nassau, right were the last remembered being, sitting on a homemade chair, propped against a makeshift hut. Still in the shade, same sails dotting the horizon. He'd merely fallen asleep, but never before had he experienced a dream so real, but if he were to ask for one, a vision of the future with a beautiful woman was more than he deserved to experience. Dusting himself off, Riley reached up to adjust his hat.

It was gone.

Riley spun in place as if the wind had pulled it from his head, but he found nothing. He checked for nearby footprints from the thief, but the wind had already obscured them. Such a shame. He liked that hat.

How much time had he lost? Did Vallo sneak onto his *Angelfish* while he'd napped like a child? Riley crossed the soft sand and returned to The Golden Macaw. After allowing his eyes to adjust, he searched the room. Only a few patrons milled about quietly. His crew was gone. Many of the crew knew of his favorite resting location. Why didn't they rouse him before leaving?

Riley approached the owner who'd taken over behind the bar. She promptly turned and smiled broadly for him. Her voluptuous stature commanded attention, and her curls piled high were of the most distinguished taste. Everyone respected Marta, and since she had sharp ears when her bar was filled with loose lips, they also listened to her.

"Aye, my Riley. Where've you been?" She grinned while cleaning out a mug.

"I'm looking for my crew. Have you seen them?" Riley leaned against the bar and smiled to charm the information out of her.

Looking at her mug, she tilted her head. "I've been hearin' 'em. You lost two captains to women, the word says. Sounds like your crew is cursed, and you're next." She pointed at him with a rag.

Riley thought of his dream, but that was impossible. He knew where his end would be, and nothing could change that. "I don't believe in such things."

Marta set down the mug and tossed the rag on the bar. Her hand rested on her hip. "People pour through my doors like sand and glide out like the tide. I'm here to keep the mugs full, and they go about their business, renderin' me invisible. But I see you." She gestured for him to take a seat and then returned that hand to her hip.

No one defied the orders from the lady of the house. Riley sat on a stool across from her.

"For years you've been comin' here on shore leave," she continued. "When the haul's good, you've got an empty smile on your lips, but when its bad, the smile is the same. You're not after the prize."

He couldn't argue with that, but he was curious where she was going with this. "What's it matter?"

"If your heart's not in it, get out before the men learn your interests don't align. Some of them already been whispering."

Vallo intended to raise a ruckus on board, but Riley tensed at her usage of the plural. "Oh?"

"You don't want to be on that ship anymore, so quit. Stay here. Find yourself a woman and live the life you've been wantin'. Not such a bad way to go, endin' things like that. A woman on the arm is better than a noose around the neck."

Frustrated with the useless information, Riley said, "I'll take your advice into account, but I doubt its value."

"Well, I hate to see a good man flounder."

"Marta, where's my crew?" Riley's tone was sharper than he intended, and he stood, not wanting to waste more time.

The plump woman dipped her chin and raised her brow. "From the chatter I heard, they was headed to the ship. Mighty excited, they were."

Riley slapped the bar's surface. Finally, something he could use. "Thanks, ma'am."

She nodded with a grim set to her mouth.

Riley set off through town to the docks, sand slowing his every frustrated step. How could Marta suggest he walk away from the captaincy and stay here, a dull life on a despicable island of sand and sweat? That was worse than what he already had. Besides, what kind of woman would accept a pirate like him?

The only woman who piqued his interest and didn't despise him was merely a dream, an illusion. Miss Robin Hall. Riley didn't believe in curses, and he didn't need to yearn for something impossible. Allowing his hopes to soar only ended in a pain he refused to repeat.

Riley already had his plan, and his crew was in danger. All her warnings and useless advice were nothing but distractions.

At the dock, various men loaded and unloaded boats for the market, many of which participated willingly in the island's illicit trade, including Riley when the occasion called for it. Shielding his eyes from the harsh sun glaring off the water's surface, Riley identified ship after ship by the markings on the sails or the names scrawled on the hulls. None were enemies—that he was aware of—-and none were his. Still, he kept searching, squinting against the light. One single-masted sloop, a fishing vessel, sailed forward. The *Angelfish* anchored slightly beyond, bringing Riley's lips into a grin. He wasn't too late. Rushing down the dock, Riley found Cantu climbing aboard a longboat and two rowers with him.

"Good of you to continue working," Riley said to their backs. "Are we refitted and ready to cast off?"

Cantu turned and smiled. "Captain! We thought we lost you to the brothel. No one could find you!"

"How is the account coming along?"

"Ship's restocked for the voyage across the Atlantic. We recruited two dozen men willing to sail with us."

A total of four dozen. Probably not enough, but more than he'd expected. "Excellent."

"Come along, captain. This is the last boat over." Cantu gestured for him to join them.

With one last look at Nassau, Riley climbed in. Would he see this town again? Would he visit the bar and brothel again? How many of his crew would survive this perilous course? He'd do whatever it took to make his crew richer than they'd ever dreamed. Starting with keeping his crew in good spirits despite the odds stacked against them. Riley didn't need encouragement. He knew where his end would be found. Picturing his future-brother-in-law and his betrothed, Riley smiled.

Soon.

The row over to the *Angelfish* was efficient. As an English schooner, her draft was shallow, at a mere five feet. She could anchor much closer to shore than most ships of her size, an advantage during escapes, and although she was outfitted stronger than the *Sea Lion*, she wasn't a formidable opponent at sea. With their account chosen as a fort on an island in the middle of a broad river, that disadvantage was not a concern.

On the main deck of his ship, Riley breathed in deeply, relishing the familiar salty sea air, the humid breeze, and flapping of the sails unfurling. He was home, and after his wild dream against the shady hut, he was happier than he'd been in a while. Too bad it was only an illusion, but one which would carry his spirits until he no longer needed them.

Quartermaster John Randall approached with a status update. He read from his notes, "Fully stocked with chickens and salted pork. Giles is confident we have plenty of provisions to make the round-trip journey. Buckley and Watts say our lumber and fasteners are appropriate to manage repairs. McKee and Gunner inspected the guns. Ten serviceable guns with room for more." He chuckled at his own implication. "We currently have enough men to work the guns and satisfactory shot to concern any challenger. Price secured enough pistols and swords for every man on board. Boatswain Karl Dillon says the rigging is fit, and repair supplies and replacements are secured below deck in storage. Hodgens is ready for your coordinates, captain."

Riley was ready to get out of port. He smiled at Randall's optimism. *Any* challenger was an untruthful boast, but their odds of encountering a man-o'-war was slim. "Excellent work, Randall. Send word for William Price to meet me in the navigation room."

"At once, captain." Randall was an excellent quartermaster, as he'd claimed. Strong, sturdy, and thorough. But as Randall was not known long, and remembering Marta's warning, Riley chose his words with care and kept his distance.

Riley pushed through the navigation room door, where Hodgens made repairs to his own cocked hat. Riley glanced at it wistfully. He should've detoured for a replacement.

"Captain, a pleasure to see you've returned to us." Hodgens placed his hat on his head and stood. "I'm not sure what would've come over the hungry crew if you'd been left behind. Now that you're here, we need not concern ourselves with that. Give me your coordinates, and I shall get us underway."

Riley found the paper of calculations in his pocket, and it was damaged but legible, almost like the ink had gotten wet. Strange. Until he remembered ale rained on him in celebration in the bar. Riley gave it to the man.

"Most excellent, sir." The helmsman left with a nod as William Price entered.

"You called for me, captain?"

"Close the door."

William did and approached with an unusual seriousness to his features. Unlike his younger brother, the lanky Price was quite jovial, considering his imprisonment on *Peibo del ler San Francisco* for months.

"Have you heard from Vallo?" Riley asked.

The armorer scratched at his jaw in contemplation. "Below deck, sharpening the swords with little Peter Gunner. Well, I suppose after a trip to the brothel, he's not so little anymore." Price grinned with self-satisfaction.

Riley could only focus on the enemy lurking on board under their noses. He backed up a step and scowled. "And you allowed it?"

Price dropped his levity, as if offended. "I was younger than him when I had my first—"

"Not that," Riley interrupted. "Vallo. Why is he here?"

"I wasn't aware we had issue with the man."

Riley's anger grew. The one thing Henry Price had warned him about happened, and no one else seemed concerned in the slightest. "Buckley, Cantu, and Hodgens were part of the raiding party in Cuba. They witnessed Vallo's traitorous move. They said nothing?"

"Not to me, so I had no reason to suspect him. The orders were to fill the ranks."

"I recall." Riley slid a hand down his face, clearing away an insufficient amount of sweat from his brow. "All essential roles for navigation are to proceed as planned. Everyone else is to meet on the main deck for a vote."

"Consider it done." Price nodded and stepped out.

Riley fisted the first piece of paper he found and squeezed. He didn't need extra complications with a plan already too precarious for most to attempt.

As the Angelfish unfurled her sails for the open sea, Riley turned in place, addressing the crew with his hands clasped behind his back. "Many of you are new, some of you are seasoned." Riley glared at Vallo as he made his pass. "But it has come to my attention that one among you is a traitor. Because our plan hinges entirely on trust, we cannot allow his continued presence."

The men turned their heads, mumbling to each other in confusion.

"Vallo! Step forward," Riley ordered.

The stocky man emerged from the crowd, while the crew glanced between Riley and Vallo with surprise. The traitor casually held a sword, and a look of innocence and confusion sprung across his face.

Riley knew better. "This man colluded with the prior captain to ensure the smooth operation and cooperation of this ship," he began.

"Actually, captain, that was the *Sea Lion* you're referring to," Buckley said. "We didn't have the *Angelfish* then."

Riley pinched the bridge of his nose. "Right."

"Then what's the problem?" Kerr asked, one of the new recruits. How a man accustomed to the sea could manage to keep such heft on him baffled Riley. The portly Giles was the exception. The cook spent his time preparing and tasting food, usually seated, a position most respected. But Kerr claimed to be a seasoned sailor. A decade ago, perhaps.

"The moment Captain Henry Price needed him most, Vallo, who'd been considered a trusted mate, turned his weapon on Price. He'd sold the crew's location to the enemy for a handsome reward, directly resulting in Spain's swift arrest of the crew, an action that never would've happened if Vallo's own hand hadn't betrayed us. And we lost many good men that day."

Gasps and murmurs bubbled from the crowd, but Vallo stood in front of them all casually, still holding the sword as if displaying he'd been innocently interrupted.

The game had begun.

"Do I get to defend myself, captain?" His tone was dark, a warning, and by all rights Riley should heave the man overboard, but that wouldn't win him the respect of the newest members.

Riley nodded.

Vallo addressed the crew, mirroring Riley's pacing and inflections, "It's true. The captain asked me to betray my own friends for him, and without hesitation, I agreed. And I'd do it all again, because the captain told me my actions were in the best interest of the crew as a whole. I stayed by the captain's side as his fullest supporter, until he went too far. Henry Price's own actions led directly to the crew's arrest. I stand before you now grateful for the chance to assure everyone on this ship I will do anything to benefit this crew. If the captain needs me to do his bidding, I will agree." Vallo shot Riley a dark look. "Because I have the courage to do anything, so long as we all get rich in the end."

Murmurs of agreement, shoulders lifting in dismissive shrugs, and nods worried Riley. Eyes shifted to him for a rebuttal. He addressed Vallo, "We can trust actions, not words, and as you have already proven your word means nothing, we will vote now. *Aye* for the traitor to stay. *Nay* for him to be cast overboard." The ship was still within range of shore. Provided the man could swim, this result was merely a minor inconvenience. "All those in favor of him staying?"

The *ayes* rang loudly.

"And against?"

Not nearly enough.

Vallo smirked.

With frustration boiling, Riley asked the crew, "Can I ask why you prefer to keep a traitor among you?"

"Captain," Cantu said, stepping forward. "Most of these men saw nothing of his betrayal, and more than half only met him. Vallo is a competent sailor, and you said yourself this mission requires as many hands as possible."

With a defeated sigh, Riley gestured. "Back to work. Bring us to the African coast. Hodgens, you have your coordinates."

The helmsman nodded, and the men cheered, setting about their duties. Riley retired to his cabin and sprawled on the firm mattress of his narrow bed, surprisingly tired after his nap under the palms. He hoped peaceful sleep would drag him back to Robin Hall and her wild world. He missed her, and although Riley's mind wasn't in its best place, he was not troubled by his sudden need for an illusion. Riley drifted off to sleep with more hope than he'd held in a long while.

Chapter 12

ROBIN BLINKED AND RUBBED her eyes as they adjusted to the darkness surrounding her. The only light source was a small round window in the wall—a wooden, creaking wall. A stink, reminding her of a call she'd responded to for a medical waste dumpster fire, involving junkies, used needles, and cigarettes, filled her nose and watered her eyes.

Robin coughed on the fumes, and a loud groan of wood startled her. The floor listed heavily, tossing her off balance like a drunk. Robin jutted out her hands for stability and noticed the tricorne hat in her hand. Her face twisted in confusion as she shuffled to the window.

Rolling blue waters with no land in sight. Robin rubbed her eyes again, blinked, and checked again. Nope, same waves for miles. She was on a boat.

Someone must've dragged her onto the tour ship, but how could she forget walking from the festival grass to this pungent pile of wood? She hadn't drunk anything that could've been spiked. Her fingers pressed against the back of her head. She wasn't hit either. It made no sense. Her feet itched to run back to land, but only seeing water ahead of her, the odds of making that work were slim.

Robin hated boats, but it wasn't because of seasickness.

Years had passed since Robin had last been on a boat, which had been a slow pontoon and nothing like this ancient behemoth. Robin wouldn't have gone on this ship voluntarily—regardless of Emily's pleading, so this had to be a nightmare. She'd slept terribly last night—or not at all, actually, so she'd dozed off after driving home from the festival this morning. The theory made sense.

After Riley had left, she'd tossed and turned, thinking about him. Worrying? Yeah, she worried. So much so, she drove around half the night looking for him, and after a nap, she'd hunted the festival grounds for him. Had she dozed off *while* driving? For all she knew, Robin was comatose in a hospital after a car crash, and this nightmare-inducing ship was a trip to the unexplored gray matter of her temporal lobe, helped along by IV drugs.

Robin's brain, with nothing better to do, was testing her, but she glanced at Riley's hat in her hand. Perhaps not a test, but a tease. A taste of what Riley had described to her. A flash of his life.

That was all crap.

Emily must've dragged her on here, and complete terror had her blacking out the boarding process. Did Robin have the strength to survive this pungent ride on Lake Michigan and make it back to the festival?

Only one way to find out.

Robin used her hands for balance as she shuffled her way out of the nauseating room packed with barrels. Through the doorway, she found an open space where hammocks hung from the low ceiling. They swayed with the ship's movement. Lined up against the exterior walls were long, black tubes of some sort. She couldn't make them out. A beam of light shined on a staircase in the center of the strange room. Fighting the floor rocking under her feet, Robin rushed to the ladder and gripped it with one hand while hugging Riley's hat with the other. She stopped.

She held Riley's hat. The crazy pirate captain who'd appeared at the festival and vanished from her apartment. The sexy man who'd said her mom's death wasn't her fault.

Riley was never real.

Robin's grief conjured him to attempt to bring her absolution in her mom's murder. And as she stood here now, holding the imaginary Riley's hat, standing at the foot of a ladder with light shining down, on a terrifying boat, Robin had only one answer.

In complete exhaustion, chasing an imaginary being, she had crashed her car. This nightmare scene was her subconscious pushing her toward the light.

To find relief.

To escape her grief.

To escape.

But climbing toward the light meant dying, as she understood it, and like any healthy person, she didn't want to die. Robin glanced around herself. If this was some sort of in-between the living and the afterlife, where was her messenger? Wasn't someone supposed to give her guidance on which way to go? If climbing the ladder meant dying, how did she return to her body?

How did she fight back?

Releasing the ladder, Robin turned around and searched the darkened space. She approached one of the black tubes and pushed on the square outlined on the wall in front of it. A series of ropes and pulleys shifted. The square moved.

Light showed her the tube was a...cannon? Two tidy rows of cast iron cannons hugged the exterior walls.

A dreadful thought popped into her mind. She wasn't religious in the slightest, but was this purgatory? Had the ancient texts been right? Was she going to hell next? She hadn't lived long enough to justify dying this young. She'd learned the painful lesson that life wasn't fair, but knowing that truth was easier than accepting it. What had she done that was so terrible?

She'd failed to save her mom from a burglar and she'd died.

She'd failed to save Clark Thompson from a robber and he'd died.

Why couldn't she go back and make it right?

With nerves tensing her stomach, Robin peered through the square trap door. More waves of water greeted her. This was definitely not a tease of Riley before her final destination; this was definitely a test.

Robin turned around, facing the light shining down on the ladder. There was no way out, no guardian, no last words of comfort or advice. There was only up.

The ship bucked under the waves, and a spray of water hit her on the back. With a cringe, Robin stood and repositioned her purse over her shoulder and hugged the hat. At least she had her Glock—a small comfort. The only comfort...

No, that wasn't right. Someone would be up there to greet her. Robin smiled, and a warmth of relief flooded her chest. Tears stung her eyes, and she swallowed back the pressing emotion. Dying wasn't all bad.

Holding her arm out for balance, she crossed to the ladder and gripped it tight. Wood creaked overhead. Footsteps thundered.

"I'm coming, Mom."

Robin climbed the ladder into the light.

Robin Hall's eyes widened as men scurried all around her, pulling and tying lines, while others climbed skyward—a flurry of activity she couldn't begin to understand. Where...where was her mom? The smile vanished. The tears dried up. The ship listed, tugging Robin to the side of the opening, and she gripped the rim of the damp deck with her hat-free hand, but she slipped. A prick of her finger had her pull away. Robin inspected her injury. A splinter, tiny and insignificant, but real enough.

She bled.

This wasn't the afterlife she'd expected. The test wasn't over. She needed to prove to herself she could escape her mind's game and return to her body, which based on the setting given to her, meant getting off this ship and returning to the festival—a metaphor her brain conjured because of Riley's wild stories. Survive this game. Return home. Face the consequences of the irresponsible crash she'd caused by being severely sleep deprived. She hoped no one else was hurt because of her.

"Stowaway!" a man yelled behind her.

Robin followed the voice, and a hand with several missing fingers pointed at her. A scowling face on an emaciated body accompanied it. He seemed so real. Frankly, Robin was surprised at her mind's creativity.

"I'm not a stowaway." Robin played along, digging in the pockets of her skinny jeans and finding nothing. She unzipped her purse and fished around for a ticket. She didn't have one. "Maybe I am. I don't know. I'm sorry. Is that the right answer?"

"Look at her clothes, Landry." Another man, hefty around the middle with a stained outfit straight from a historical movie, said to the first. He looked like the type of man Robin would request backup for, a man who wouldn't play nice or listen to authority.

"Don't need to, Kerr," Landry with the missing fingers said. "Rules demand stowaways go overboard."

Overboard? Why did her subconscious feel the need to punish herself further? The possibility she hurt or killed someone in the crash returned. Robin swallowed that terrible thought and repeated her plan: Survive first, beg forgiveness after, and serve out whatever sentence was handed to her last.

"I didn't mean to, I swear. Please take me to land, and I'll pay you whatever I owe, plus interest."

Robin met the gazes of each man around her. No one said anything. One folded his arms across his chest. Several raked their eyes along her body. Rough men, indeed. Precisely the men she wouldn't envision if this were a dream, confirming this was a test. With a voice pleading for a deal, she added, "And a tip? A big tip?"

"Overboard!" Another man shouted from the back.

"Hold on there," a short, stocky man pushed forward. His dark eyes met her gaze, and he reached out a hand. "The name's Vallo. How do you do, ma'am?"

Robin could play hardball with her own mind, and to show herself how much she hated this game, Robin left Vallo's hand hanging. One, it was filthy. Two, she didn't trust any of these men—imagined or not.

Vallo leaned down and took her hand, anyway. Before she could tug out of his grip, he flipped her hand over and kissed her knuckles. Robin recoiled from his touch and rubbed her knuckles clean on her jeans.

"I'll do better when I get home, I swear. You need to turn this ship around." She checked her knuckles to be sure the germs were gone.

Men laughed and murmured to each other.

Yeah, okay. She couldn't rub germs off.

Vallo's calculating eyes landed on Riley's hat in her hand, and a devious smile stretched his lips. "We need to consult the captain. Aye, we need him to see this."

"Captain takes all the fun out of it," Landry countered. "Lady, I hope you know how to swim." The smirking sneer on his gaunt face told her too much. She could swim, but glancing at the horizon in all directions, that skill was pointless. She hated boats, and now she couldn't escape. What kind of test would be impossible to complete?

That flash of nerves formed into a heavy rock.

"Wait, wait," another man in the front of the crowd said, holding out his hands in a placating gesture. He smiled at Robin, displaying yellowed and blackened teeth. Robin held back a cringe. Despite his revolting appearance, at least the man had some decency to defend her against these ridiculous requests. "We want her naked first."

Guess not.

Piggish laughter and a wave of agreement rolled through the crowd. On her own turf, Robin could handle herself well. Even on this listing imaginary ship, she could subdue a few of these men with no problem. But this many was definitely a problem. Despite Vallo standing up for her, briefly, she didn't think he'd raise a hand against his own colleagues.

Robin had brought her Glock, but these men didn't appear to be susceptible to intimidation. She was trained to shoot for the kill, since an injured suspect was still a dangerous one. If she caused the death of one of these men, none of the rest seemed likely to surrender. And shooting all of them would leave no one to sail the ship back to the festival.

This entire scenario rested on her ability to pull the trigger in the first place. If that wasn't an obvious test wrapped straight around the writhing pain in her heart, she didn't know what was. Even if that was the answer—stand up and fire—she couldn't. Not with this many men. No one on earth was that fast at shooting and reloading, and Robin hadn't brought enough mags.

Completion of the test had to be something else. Something more subtle.

A man pawed at the neckline of her T-shirt. Without thinking, Robin struck downward at his elbow, flinging his arm off her. At once, her pulse kicked into gear, ready to defend herself. The perpetrator's smiling face fell with surprise and concealed pain.

Another grabbed at her waist, and with a grunt, she kicked him in the knee. Her chest lifted and fell with rapid breaths, adrenaline surging at the unprovoked attack, and whatever remained to come next. On a barrel behind her, Robin set down Riley's hat, a symbol of her subconscious she wouldn't ignore. She raised her arms in a boxer's stance, and the men backed up a step.

"Seems we caught ourselves a slippery fish, mates." Kerr said with a devious grin. Clearly, he wasn't planning on challenging her next.

"What kind of game is this?" Robin asked, mostly to herself. Perhaps asking out loud would encourage her mind to respond directly through the mouths of these men. She held her arms at the ready, in case her brain didn't like that question.

The men exchanged confused looks.

Why would her brain be confused by her own question?

"What's going on over here?" A thin, black-haired older man pushed through the pungent crowd. This one was missing teeth too. His bushy brows lifted when he laid eyes on Robin, and a flash of recognition at Riley's hat on the barrel confused her. "I see. Green, Landry, Kerr, the rest of you scurvy dogs, get back to work!" he addressed the men, most of which listened. They scattered to their roles and resumed whatever they were told, but Kerr and Landry hung back.

"We have a woman stowaway on board, Buckley, and you want us to ignore her?" Kerr asked in disbelief.

"That's right. You heard my orders."

"Unbelievable," Landry said, anger burning on his face. "This ship lives up to its reputation. The prize better be worth it."

Kerr and Landry walked away, whispering to each other. Only this Buckley fellow remained. Assessing his strength and casual posture, she relaxed her fighting stance. He meant her no harm. Robin picked up Riley's hat, a security blanket of sorts. She wouldn't read too deeply into that.

"Another one of you, eh? The curse is real." Buckley shook his head in amusement. "You're lucky Cantu, I, and a couple others have been through this show before, otherwise those dirty dogs would've had their way with you, and I suppose a few dozen others."

Robin scowled.

"No worries, lady. You see that door over there?" Buckley pointed to the only door at the stern of the ship.

Robin nodded.

"Introduce yourself." Buckley, the old man of the ship, smiled slyly and turned away.

Robin pressed Riley's hat to her chest while she crossed the rocking ship. Angry eyes glared back at her from all sides and above. The masts must've reached a hundred feet in the air, and from way down here, she couldn't see any safety harnesses on the men. Despite her recent status as an unemployed police officer, public safety was her biggest priority, so her mind should've placed harnesses on them. Then again, her mind allowed her to crash her car while sleep deprived. She couldn't even trust herself.

Okay, subconscious, bring on the next section of the test.

At the creaking wood door, Robin lifted her fist and knocked.

13

Chapter 13

Captain Noah Riley groggily pulled himself to a seated position on his mattress, knocking a bottle of rum onto the floor. The heavy glass thumped and rolled to the wall with the sway of the ship. He pressed his fingertips to his throbbing temples and rubbed. After a quick glance around the room to judge its position, Riley determined the drink had worn off. Shame. He stretched his neck and shoulders with a soft groan and bent and retrieved the bottle. It was empty.

Bigger shame.

Riley sighed. They were weeks from Nassau and days from their target on the Gambia River. His private stash was now gone, and he couldn't take from the crew without dire consequences. Each day he'd checked in with Hodgens, and once he was satisfied with their coordinates and progress, Riley returned to his private cabin and indulged in the tart rum. He'd never been much of a drinker, since needing to keep his wits strong and alert were critical of a captain, but now he couldn't stay away from it.

Every day and every night he hoped for a chance to see Robin Hall again. She had brought him peace from the faces haunting his thoughts, and for that, he was eternally grateful. But no matter his efforts, the only place her gentle face existed was in his awake mind. As the days passed, he began to wonder if he could keep the details of her alive. Would the wisps of her dark hair go first or the tantalizing hem of her blouse? Could he hold on to the precise stitching of her tight breeches and the strange tangle of laces on her shoes?

Or her soft lips when they twisted in confusion?

Or her searing touch as she caressed the chain on his neck?

Oh, when that white fluffy towel was all that stood between him and her. How could he have imagined such an impossibly soft fabric? Wherever the inspiration came from, he couldn't let it go.

Riley tilted his head back. Aye, grateful for the new haunt.

A knocking on his door turned his head, but no one yelled in alarm, which meant no one was injured, dying, dead, or overboard, and they hadn't spotted sails on the horizon. Taking his time, Riley blew out a heavy breath and shrugged into his vest, tightening it over his tunic, and he checked his weapons in his bandolier. The last thing he needed was to be caught unarmed with an unstable crew. They'd already voted to keep the traitor on board, who knew what other foolish actions they were capable of.

The knocking repeated.

Riley mumbled frustrations to himself and dragged his heavy feet across the cabin. A list of the ship had him tilting off balance. He rubbed his eyes, wishing to return to sleep. Even snarling at the man interrupting him was too much effort. Riley opened the cabin door with a slack face.

He blinked twice and rubbed his eyes again. He looked over his shoulder at the empty bottle of rum and skimmed his eyes around the room. It wasn't spinning or tilting in any way out of the ordinary. Certainly he was sober. Well, sober enough to believe what his eyes showed him existed, right? Had his deep desire to hold on to her memory brought her forth from the caverns of his mind into his reality?

Looking over her shoulder, he checked the manners and behaviors of his nearby crew. No one glanced at or acknowledged her.

She stood here directly from his imagination, carrying that same look of confusion he knew so well. A t-shirt hugged her pleasant chest, and pants so tight he could see every curve on her body. He'd done it. The rum had granted his wish, and he had no intention of letting her go. Not knowing if his mind would direct her where he wanted her to go, he gestured for her to enter.

She did.

Riley closed the door behind her to prevent the crew from seeing him talking to himself. The last thing he needed was the crew more upset this close to their last prize.

She turned to face him, holding his lost hat. His favorite hat. At that thought, she held it out to him. He didn't want to take it. He feared reaching out would only confirm she was an apparition. He wanted to believe she was real.

"Riley?" Robin asked, confusion twisting her features as her arm continued to hang in the air. "Am I dead?"

What a dreadful thought. Was that the secret to her appearance? She'd chosen him to haunt for eternity. If that be the outcome, he was happy to see her. The corner of his lips lifted in a solemn smile. "I hope not."

Robin gently placed his hat on his mattress. Her fingers released the worn leather, and with bated breath, Riley stared at it, waiting for the crushing moment both the hat and Robin disappeared forever.

Robin approached him and tears pricked at his eyes, but he couldn't peel them away from the hat.

"Are you okay?" Robin leaned in close, scrutinizing his face with worry on her brow. "Your shave. How did it grow in so fast?"

As much as he relished this moment, he knew it could never last. He needed to rip out the splinter now before the pain overtook him at a terrible time—between a crew's argument, in the middle of a battle, or during the confrontation of the impending prize. He had to face the truth. Riley held up his palm.

"What are you doing?" Robin frowned.

"Humor me."

Robin mirrored with her palm in the air.

Riley dashed away tears warping his vision and reached forward slowly. Fighting against the desire to remain blind to the truth, he persisted; he had to know, even if his actions caused her to disappear forever. With a last-second shaky breath, his palm closed the distance. A solid and warm hand with soft skin pressed against his. Disbelief loosened his body, and Riley's fingers wrapped around her hand and pressed it against his chest. The weight against his body sent a wave of relief barreling against him, and he could hardly stand. He closed his eyes, pushing away the remaining tears.

"How? How is this possible?" he asked, meeting her worried gaze. "You're here. You've answered my call and come to me."

Robin's hand stayed firm, grounding him. "I don't understand. Is this...heaven?"

Most certainly not. A wet chuckle breached his throat. "The Atlantic Ocean, last I checked. By now, east of the Cabo Verde islands."

"So, not a test," she said absently. "A tease. Only a final tease." Tears formed on her lids, and Riley swiped them away with his thumb.

"It's my turn to bear the confusion."

"Last I remember, I was heading to my car. I'd been worried about you all night, so I didn't sleep much. I must've crashed, and now I'm dreaming I'm here in your world. I don't know if I'm destined to wake up and face the consequences of driving unsafely, or if this is my final goodbye. I must've called you into my subconscious to ease my crossing. But the details—the smell—are so real. It doesn't make any sense. I need to know, after you left my apartment, did you make it home safely?"

Riley opened his mouth to answer.

Robin slipped her hand free of his touch, and the warmth left his body. She gestured to stop him from answering, and she stepped away from him. "No, no don't tell me. I can't have that reassurance, or I'll be sent away. I want to believe where I'm going is the land of peace and love. I need to know my mom's waiting for me." A wistful smile lifted her beautiful mouth. "But I can't go. Not yet. So don't give me that solace."

Riley replayed her words while recalling the framed image of a woman at Robin's bedside. He remembered the details of her mother's untimely passing. Robin's fraught rambling now made sense.

Robin thought she was dying.

Why would Riley's mind invent such a heartbreaking twist for a headstrong and beautiful woman who treated him like a man, rather than a dog? Her touch felt real. She wasn't visibly injured, only lost and confused, something he'd been intimately familiar with two weeks ago.

The truth of their situation dawned on him as details popped into his head. Prior to the previous captain stepping down, Henry Price had warned Riley about women traveling in time. Although Riley had met the unusual Emily Porter and Angela Foxe, he dismissed the idea as nonsense.

Was it possible that not only had Riley done it when he'd met Robin, but that she somehow followed him back here? There was one way to know for sure.

Riley closed the cold distance between them, heart pounding in his chest. He couldn't lose what he'd gotten back. "You're not dying."

Robin met his gaze and frowned. "What?"

To help ground her, he lifted his palm again. She reached for it quickly this time, and he gripped her tight. "There's a connection between us; we are linked together. As I was in your world, you are now in mine."

Robin tilted her head and scrunched her nose in thought.

"You're standing on the *Angelfish*," he added.

"How could I imagine...?" Robin trailed off as the thoughts in her head showed on her face, and Riley held her like a lifeline.

"You didn't. I'm not in your head, as you are not in mine. We are both real, and we're both here. I can prove it to you."

Robin looked at their clasped hands. "How?"

Riley gently cupped her neck and leaned down. He slowly brought his lips to hers, for if he was wrong, this would be the one and only kiss. Closing his eyes, he pressed against hers. Heat, like the incredible hot shower pouring over his body, once again rushed through his limbs, and pooled down low. His breeches tightened as their lips changed position, and he released her hand and pulled her against his body, against her lips, leaning into her. Desperation for her touch swallowed him whole. Desperation for this to be real kept him kissing her. He couldn't stop. He couldn't open his eyes and have all this torn from him again.

Robin's arms wrapped around his neck, demanding he stay close, and that was a wish he would grant over and over. Riley grasped Robin's hips and pressed her against his hard length, growing with the need to be inside her.

Something hard pressed back.

"Ow," he exclaimed unintentionally. He pulled back and looked down at Robin.

She followed his gaze to the sack between them. "It's my gun." Her chest lifted and fell, and she twisted the bag to her back. "Where were we?"

"You were deciding if I'm real."

Robin smiled deviously, sending heat surging through his body once again. "I haven't decided yet."

The cabin door flung wide with a screech, startling them both. Armorer William Price split the doorway with his lanky frame. "So it's true, Captain."

"Captain?" Robin whispered to herself, as if finally believing what he'd told her was the truth.

He couldn't help a prideful lift of his lips. As she was realizing the full gravity of the truth he'd given her, Riley was realizing Robin Hall was really here.

Price glanced at Robin. "You found our stowaway. How much longer are women going to keep infiltrating our ships? Like rats, they keep popping up no matter how many you dispatch."

Robin whispered, "Rats?"

With impatience, Riley asked, "What business do you have, Price?"

The armorer shook his head in bewilderment. "As you know, I have no interest in the trappings of the fairer sex—"

"Trappings?" Robin repeated on a whisper.

Riley didn't respond to her aggravation, primarily because she could handle herself, but also Riley understood Price's stance on women: He wanted nothing to do with them. And while Price was still a fair and trustworthy man, many sailors on this ship were not. Riley listened closely to his armorer's concerns.

"But the rumor of another skirt on deck has the crew in a fuss. The newest recruits aren't aware of our unusual history. If you want to keep her to yourself, you must assert your position."

Not a problem. "I shall address the crew. In the meantime, you'll do well to insist they have nothing to worry about."

"It's not their worries that concern me." Price shot a look at Robin.

More troublemakers. When Angela had appeared on the *Sea Lion*, Vallo, along with his best friends, Berger and Liverman, were the biggest noise on the ship, rallying the crew against Henry Price. The latter two were dead, but the former? The biggest thorn in Riley's side.

"Was Vallo one of the instigators?" Riley asked.

"No, sir. Haven't seen him."

If that wasn't surprising, Riley didn't know what would be.

"I saw Vallo," Robin said. "He introduced himself."

That would do it.

"Thank you for your council, Price," Riley said in dismissal.

The armorer closed the door, and Riley blew out a breath. No longer worried over the crew's opinions on his uncharacteristic imbibing, now he had someone special to take care of, a responsibility he both relished and feared. The biggest worry he could've imagined.

"You were calling his name at the festival," Robin added. "What's so alarming about this Vallo guy?"

"He's someone you'd do best to avoid." Riley took in the sight of her scandalous clothing and said, "As much as I enjoyed the *shapeliness* of your world, let's get you out of those clothes, they shall only add to their case here. And so you understand your predicament, only McKee, Giles, Price, Buckley, Cantu, Karl, and Hodgens are trustworthy."

"You expect me to remember all those names?"

"If any of them talk to you, ask their name. If it's familiar, they're likely safe," Riley said with a gentle smile.

"I recognize one. Buckley sent me in here."

Just like the old coot. "And as such, you're lucky. Your presence on this ship is forbidden, and by all rights you must answer to the crew."

"How?"

Riley saw no gain in lying to her. "The typical punishment is marooning. Since neither you nor I want that, a wise choice is for you to blend in. Convince the crew you are one of them, regardless of the status of your breast. Here in my trunk I have extra clothes. I'm sure something will be suitable." Riley leaned down and lifted his hat. "Thank you for returning it to me. It's my favorite hat."

Robin smiled in response and kneeled at his trunk. She picked through his spare clothes, lifting garments and looking at them closely. One was a fancy dress which she promptly returned.

Captain Riley couldn't believe she was here before him, now sharing his world as he shared hers, and she handled the change much better than he had. But his smile of gratitude at his good fortune slid away. Riley was leading the crew into a perilous raid, so perilous, in fact, he had no intention of surviving it. He wanted her nowhere near this prize, but he couldn't leave her behind on the ship either, when the majority of the crew wanted her dead.

Chapter 14

Cloudy skies brought relief to Robin's tired eyes. An ache of exhaustion tugged at her eyelids, but now was not the time for rest, because if she did anything wrong in the next few minutes, she'd be resting permanently at the bottom of the Atlantic.

In her short-lived career as a police officer, sometimes Robin had to take the stand as an expert to give testimony or as a material witness in a case. Within those parameters, a set of defined procedures to moving a person of interest through the legal process was...mostly clear. But here, where she was miraculously alive with Riley at her side, Robin felt like not only was she on a high-profile murder trial, but that the judge, jury, and executioner had a personal bone to pick with her.

Instead of wearing her department blues and holding her head high, or her street clothes and having a sense of self, Robin formally stood before the crew, but now her clothes were uncomfortable, ill-fitting, and yeah, they smelled like salty fish. For whatever reason, many of these men hated her.

Standing at her side, Riley sent her a sorrowful smile while the quartermaster paced around the interested crew. When she'd arrived on this nightmarish boat, she thought she was being tested by her subconscious to see if she had what it took to return to her body and make amends for whatever damage she'd caused in her car accident, but once she saw Riley, she knew it had to be a tease instead. One last reward before traveling over the rainbow bridge.

Then he kissed her...that was real.

Noah Riley wasn't an escaped mental patient from somewhere in England. Here he was no longer scared, lost, or rambling on about impossibilities. Everything he'd said about the Crown's unfairness, all his confusion about vehicles and food, all his excitement over a refrigerator, electricity, and running water were genuine. A man from a different time, who'd crossed not only once, but twice. And somehow, she'd followed him.

Riley had told her he was the captain of the *Angelfish*, but the way the quartermaster and the crew scowled at her and Riley, she wondered what power the captain had. And the flag flying on the masthead was an English symbol, not 'the black'. As he had been confused about her world, she was lost about his. She should've spent more time listening to Emily's tales of the past.

Robin hadn't crashed her car. She wasn't dying at all. She still believed this was a test, but an entirely different one. This wasn't to cleanse her subconscious of guilt. This was survival.

"Upon our decks, we have a stowaway," Quartermaster Randall said, holding his hands behind his back and pacing like a military officer. "Upon our hearts, we have the articles. An agreement we all signed to ensure the proper behavior and mutual agreement of all those on board. One among us did not sign, nor was granted permission to board. In fact, this person stole from us."

The crew murmured to each other, and the tone settled a pressure on Robin's shoulders.

When they quieted down, the quartermaster continued, "Our agreement is clear. Any stowaway is to be marooned. Any accusation of thievery is to be satisfied by a duel on shore."

This time the murmurs grew into excitement.

"There is one additional factor to consider. Our stowaway is a woman, and Captain Riley would like to say a few words before the decision is handed down."

Riley left her side and took up the center of attention. "Everyone, this is Robin Hall, my personal guest. My sincerest apologies for not announcing her presence sooner."

The scowls turned in her direction, and Robin hugged her arms.

"Where's she been hidin'?" a voice called out.

Riley turned to face the questioning man. "Does that matter?"

The man glowered.

"No one is to harm Robin. Anyone who attempts to lay a finger on her shall answer to me personally." Riley sent her a wink. His confidence, assertiveness, and public declaration defending her sent a rush of heat scorching her veins. As he strolled along the deck, addressing all the men, she pictured his naked form and wished she'd taken a better look. That visual softened the pressure from her shoulders. This sexy, strong man was going to save her from these pigs.

"This ship ain't that big, captain. How did she get past all our checks?"

This man's statement was more an observation than an accusation, and the captain smiled.

"It's the curse, don't you see?" another answered. "This ship is cursed!"

The crew mumbled its concern.

The man with the missing fingers, Landry, stepped forward. "What curse? I wasn't told nothing about no curse."

"Aye, a curse be an important factor in signing the articles," the hefty Kerr said, stepping up to Landry's side.

"If this ship's cursed, we want a bigger share, captain," a man with yellow and blackened teeth said, standing with his upset friends.

Riley faced the three of them. "What share do you deem fair, Green?"

The unsightly Green conferred with Kerr and Landry briefly. One of the men grinned in a way that sent shivers down Robin's back. Breaking their huddle, Green said, "If we're taking the risk of a woman on board, then what's fair is we all get a turn with 'er."

Most of the crew cheered. Buckley, who'd sent Robin to the captain, didn't. Neither did a very large man. A portly fellow with a stained apron also looked solemn, as did the helmsman. Five men against a crew of what...dozens?

Robin swallowed a dry lump in her throat.

Riley spun on his men, face flushing red, and his body clenched for action. The situation had escalated, and Riley intended to take them all on. For her. Worry gripped her chest as she remembered his attempt to fight a parked car. She had been able to subdue him easily.

"Randall, care to control your men?" Riley asked through gritted teeth.

The quartermaster smirked and motioned for the crew to settle down. When they quieted, Robin exhaled in relief.

"This isn't how we settle things on this ship," Randall said to the captain. "If one of us starts breaking the rules, then we all will, and then we no longer have an account. Agreeing to the articles is what keeps us whole and functional. As representative of this crew, by their vote I remind you, I cannot allow such disregard for the rules to stand, despite extenuating circumstances. We are two days at most from the mouth of the Gambia River. This is the worst time for you to spring such betrayal on us."

Riley tensed. "Be careful with your accusation, Randall. I did not stash a woman in my cabin for weeks. As you can see, she's clean and nourished. Giles, you never brought extra rations to my cabin?" Riley addressed the wide fellow with an apron, who promptly shook his head.

"And as I am still in a healthful shape," Riley added, "I have not shared my rations."

"You've been drinking a lot, captain. No need for extra rations if you've got rum for fuel," Landry said.

Riley spun with barely contained rage. "I'm telling the truth. If you believe her appearance to be the result of a curse of good fortune, then we are in agreement. But accusing me of betrayal is a serious offense. Robin is one of us. She will dine with us, assist the crew, and pull her own weight." Riley glanced at Robin with pity in his eyes. That was unnecessary. Robin could handle herself, and if climbing around this ship was all it took to keep these brutes pacified, so be it.

"Pretending to be an equal doesn't make her one," the quartermaster argued.

This guy didn't know a thing about Robin, but he assumed she was useless and helpless. What was wrong with these men?

"That's a fair statement," Riley said, and Robin shot him a look. Riley winked, indicating he had other plans, so Robin trusted him to stand up for her. "Since you have vitriol under your skin, for her safety, Robin will share my cabin."

The crew erupted with anger.

Robin stiffened, and Riley returned to her side and whispered in her ear, "They don't accept change well."

"Clearly. Now what? How are we going to argue against all of them?" Even if those few allies stood up against the rest of the crew, would they fight for her, or would they back down at the first threat? She didn't know any of these men.

"They need time."

Robin didn't understand. "You're the captain. Can't you order them to calm down? Can't you tell them to leave me alone?"

A flicker passed over his features. "The captain holds ultimate power during battle, and he leads the crew on the account. When it comes to matters of the crew, the quartermaster is their voice. A balance of power, if you will."

As the men raged, nothing looked balanced here.

Randall quieted the crew. "I need not remind you of my position. As the crew has come to an agreement by their voices, Robin will not share your cabin. If you disagree, we will find ourselves with a problem."

Riley's fists squeezed until his knuckles blanched. Robin wanted to stay by his side. If she couldn't, where was she going to go? What was the crew going to do with her? Too many 'what ifs' left her stomach unsettled.

"Sails!" a voice shouted from above.

THE AGREEMENT WITH RANDAL against Captain Riley persisted until the warning call repeated. The crew calmed down, and Riley crossed the deck to the rail and pressed a spyglass to his eye. With a grim set to his mouth, he said, "Spanish merchant ship."

Riley handed the spyglass to Randall. Seconds ago, they were at each other's throats, but now they worked together, and the rest of the crew ignored her.

Randall viewed through the spyglass. "Southeast by south. She's a couple hours away. Do we risk taking this prize?" Randall asked, deferring the power to Riley, as the captain had explained to her. He returned the spyglass to Riley, who took another look.

"She's armed. Likely has valuable cargo to warrant such guns. If we can add to our supply of weaponry, I think our odds will be that much better."

Odds for what?

Nerves swirled in Robin's gut. She hugged her purse against her chest. Merchant ship meant friendly, right?

Riley faced the quartermaster with a sly grin. "I say we find out what she's carrying."

Randall nodded as if Riley wanted his approval before announcing the plan to the crew. The captain faced his men and tucked away his spyglass. "Karl, get us under full sail! You heard me you dirty dogs, let out the reefs! Tighten the halyards! We're going to hunt a Spanish prize."

The men cheered and rushed to their posts. Others cleared the deck by collecting barrels and lines and stacking them away.

Robin stood still, hoping to avoid the chaos. When a man approached, she sidestepped a barrel to avoid a confrontation. These men acted like monsters around her, and if they prepared to 'hunt' a ship, whatever that meant, she didn't want the surging testosterone turned on her.

"Speed check, Gunner!" Riley ordered. Watching him take command of a ship, of dozens of men, made Robin flush with pride. He'd protected her from these men, and now they licked out of the palm of his hand. A whirlwind of activity had Robin shaking with nerves. What else had Riley explained to her that she'd dismissed as mental illness?

A lanky young man, no older than fifteen carried something tucked into his arm like a football and rushed to the rail. He and another man worked together. The man called out, "Ten knots."

"McKee," Riley said, and a bald man with a grizzly beard gestured before approaching.

"Aye, captain."

"Make sure everyone is armed. Get the gun crews below deck and ready to fire on my command," Riley said. "At our speed, we will overtake her in a couple hours, perhaps less."

The mast lined with sails overhead turned slowly, hauled by the hands of men. If the situation were different, she'd be impressed by the feat. The deck beneath her feet listed with a wave and the sun broke through the clouds.

"Sails comin' about!" A man far above their heads shouted down.

Riley faced the stern of the ship and gestured. "Raise the black!"

He'd mentioned that before. She didn't know what 'the black' was as he referred to it, but something about it rang in her memory. The English flag on the masthead was lowered in jerky movements. In its place, a black flag climbed skyward, and the wind pulled it open.

Emblazoned in the center was a white skull and crossed swords, and Robin gasped.

Pirates?

Real pirates?

"You've got to be kidding me!" Robin shouted. That was the missing piece. Captain Noah Riley commanded a *pirate* ship.

Men turned and scowled at her, but most ignored her entirely. Robin pressed a hand against her forehead and raked her fingers through her tangled locks. With her mouth hanging open and eyes wide, Robin stared at the captain with disbelief. From what she'd seen in movies and television shows, this wasn't going to be a battle—more like a slaughter—and she was stuck in the middle.

Riley approached. "Fear not, I shall keep you safe."

She pointed at the flag and remembered Riley's words at the festival, words she'd dismissed as delusions of a history fanatic. Anger and disgust charged her. "That's the black banner? You're really pirates? The real thing—enemies of all mankind, marauders of the sea, and you're going to kill all those people on that ship to steal from them?"

Riley's warmth slid away, but rather than lash out in angry defense, his shoulders slumped ever so slightly in defeat. She'd hurt him.

Good.

"The goal of the black is for them to surrender. I've been nothing but honest with you." Riley reached out for her arm.

Robin backed away from him, hand on her forehead. "This can't be happening. I can't believe this." She paced the deck, avoiding the commotion. Falling through time was hard enough to wrap her brain around, but landing on a pirate ship in the Atlantic Ocean was something else entirely. And now they prepared to kill those people because they happened to be in the area.

If Riley hadn't stood up for her, what would the crew have done to her? Took turns with her body and then tossed her overboard like spoiled meat when they bored with her? She didn't want to know what marooning was.

Her stomach churned with the movement of the water and the unease of everything around her. She hated boats. If land was in sight, she would've taken her chances with the sharks. And then what?

How would she get home?

How was she going to survive the next several hours?

She didn't know how to wield a sword...but she had her Glock.

"Robin," Riley said, catching up to her. "I know this is difficult to process. Believe me, I was there." A charming smile lit up his features. If he was trying to cheer her up, he failed. Robin wanted to punch him for it.

"Fearing a parked car is nothing like an impending battle to the death." Her tone was snarky and rude, but she didn't care.

"And that is how we differ. I'll take a battle any day."

Robin's features pinched with confusion, and she stared at him thoughtfully. His ridiculous choice actually made sense. This world wasn't scary to him, because it was all he knew, like her world wasn't scary to her. But that was no excuse for this, and she saw firsthand the rows of cannons below deck. "You're choosing to fight those men over there. *Your* decision. Why? Don't you own enough weapons?"

Riley rested a hand on her shoulder while busy men cast her ugly glares. Riley leaned to catch her eyes. "Never mind the crew. Listen to me, I will deal with them, but until then I need you to stay safe. Lock yourself in my cabin, and I'll come get you when it's over."

Like hell.

Chapter 15

Captain Riley had given her every detail she'd asked for, so her anger and hurt was unfounded. And that reaction, to him, was a direct punch to the heart, if such an action were possible. He'd hoped easing her into this would allow her to overcome the fears and prejudices a woman of the future held—a woman who laughed at the idea of pirates.

But things moved too fast.

Riley needed a level head to keep his men alive. They were already angry with him. Robin didn't understand how precarious their situation was, and he didn't have time to explain, if she'd even listen. Hate radiated off her like heat from a boiler. If the prize hadn't appeared when it had, Riley was certain the outcome for both her and him would've been different.

"You didn't answer me." Robin shrugged away from his touch.

"We don't have time for this."

Robin stepped forward in challenge. "Then make time."

Riley stared her down, but she refused to yield. The longer he persisted, the less time they had to prepare for battle. For her sake, whether she understood or not, Riley relaxed his stance and said calmly, "I told you the Crown took everything from us. We only take what we need to survive. Nothing more."

Robin paused to chew on his words. She asked, "Then what's all the talk about prizes?"

Riley shifted his weight, patience running dangerously thin. "Sometimes, to buy food and pay wages, we need a little more." Or a lot more, in the case of men who wished to retire from the sea and the whispers of a noose in their ears.

"You're thieves and murderers. In my city, you'd be arrested and imprisoned until your trial, which would end with your guilt and further imprisonment."

She did understand; she simply didn't approve. Riley couldn't blame her. He could hardly look at himself anymore.

"Your rules aren't much different from ours."

"Then why?" Robin's voice rose, and men glared her way. Her continued argument placed them all in further danger. "Why risk prison? Why not sail around him?"

"Her," Riley corrected. "Ships are female, and she's coming about, and we're responding. If that ship over there is aggressive in any way, we shall defend ourselves."

Robin pressed her lips thin, finally accepting.

Riley patted her shoulder. "Lock the door and don't come out for anything."

Robin nodded and wove her way to the cabin, once again earning scowls from the crew. This was the bed he'd made. Now he had to sleep in it. He waited until the sound of the lock clicked over.

She was as safe as possible...for now.

SUCH A STUBBORN, FRUSTRATING man. Robin couldn't bear to see him killed or captured and imprisoned. When she'd met him, she'd first thought he was an escaped mental patient, but after appearing in his world, for a brief while, she believed him of sound mind.

Until he ordered the attack of a nearby ship for no reason.

Now she knew he suffered from mental illness. Why else would a healthy man choose to charge headfirst into a bloody battle? More importantly, Robin couldn't stop him. She couldn't keep Riley safe from himself. Now all she could do was hope.

She wasn't good at hope.

With time to kill and her worries draining her dry, Robin paced around Riley's private quarters, looking at all the neat things of the past while her legs worked out their excess energy. She found a captain's log, which she paged through. The handwriting, although beautiful in its artistic penmanship, was hard to decipher. She found a manifest—same handwriting—and she determined he'd listed cargo and its value, and the individual crew member's accumulating balances, which were shockingly tiny. Robin didn't have an inflation calculator to determine a frame of reference for how much this stuff was worth in her dollars, but she learned they lived with very little.

Why though? Why did they choose to scrape by on the stomach-churning sea at the whimsy of the weather and the hope of finding what they needed either at landfall or by brute force? The risks seemed far too high to be worth it.

Sean Coulder, the man who'd robbed the bank. The man Robin had failed to shoot upon his exit, and her failure lead to Officer Clark Thompson's death. Like these men, Mr. Coulder risked his life for a few bucks. The result was prison for him, the death of her colleague, and mandatory therapy for her. What was the point? Why choose the more difficult path?

Her mom had chosen that path. When faced with the choice of struggling as a single mom or staying with a deadbeat boyfriend, she left. Robin hadn't understood at the time, and she remembered crying about leaving daddy, but sometimes one's values and beliefs had to drive their actions, regardless of what was easy. But in the end, her mom died, anyway. Almost like fate had stepped in.

Fate could kiss her ass.

With Riley's passionate speech about standing up against the injustices in his world, Robin could see that same drive in him. The thought of his drive ending the same as Mr. Coulder's or her mom's lingered in the back of her mind.

Resting next to a sealed inkpot, Robin found another book. It was small and narrow, almost diary sized. She lifted the lid and skimmed the text. Her eyes caught on words that stilled her heart.

My Dearest,

I have missed you for another long year. Many things have changed that you must know. Captain Lemoine retired from the sea when he met a woman. It shocked me so! The woman had been pretending to be a man for weeks, and no one caught it! She seemed lovely once we got to know her.

Lady Luck struck our ship once again, and Captain Price left us to be with his woman, a very surprising woman, a Miss Angela. Two stowaways, several weeks apart. And we have not figured out how they got on board. No one admitted to the action, so no one was properly punished.

If I see another woman brought on this ship, so help me! Only a dozen men are still on the crew since Lemoine's time. The perpetrator must be one of them, one of my trusted men. If I had known how accepting they would eventually be, I would've brought you along. I miss you dearly. I love you.

We will be together again, soon enough.

Your Captain Riley

Robin checked for a date on the page, but since she didn't know what year she'd landed in, it was useless information. What wasn't useless was knowing Riley had a woman waiting for him back home. A woman he loved.

A rock formed in her chest as tears pricked her eyes. Why was she surprised? Her luck with men was the worst, and something unexplainable brought Robin here, so how could she think falling into a man's life meant anything? Fate didn't kiss her ass. Fate slapped Robin in the face.

She should've known to keep her heart guarded when it came to the office. Sure these men shared hammocks and a mess hall instead of a copy machine, but the rules still applied. No more dating colleagues.

Robin closed the book and exhaustion pulled her eyelids. She felt like she'd been awake for more than a day, and

Riley's lumpy mattress looked inviting, like a hot cup of coffee on a cold winter's night. She sat heavily, ignoring the bounce, and collapsed onto her back. With hours to spare, Robin drifted off as tears streamed down her cheeks.

Chapter 16

SOMETHING STARTLED ROBIN AWAKE way too soon. Coffee. Where was the coffee? Peeling her tired eyes open, wood beams overhead and a pungent smell reminded her the pirate ship was not a dream, unfortunately, but that meant Riley wasn't a dream either. She knew she was awake, and that the test to clear her subconscious hadn't been real. But there was an element that was: she needed to survive and find a way home.

That very real and very crushing letter reminded her of that goal. And since she quit her job, time was of the essence.

Shouts turned her head toward the locked cabin door, and a rapid fire of thumps and scrapes, like metal dragging on wood, left her with a sinking feeling. Robin approached the door and listened. Metal clanged and crashed, like swords. Gunshots went off. Robin pulled away with a gasp.

They were in battle.

She could stand here in the relative safety of the captain's private cabin, or she could go out there and see if she could help. Riley had said the plan was to take what the crew needed from the Spanish merchant ship with no resistance, but based on the sounds penetrating the thick door, a frightening level of resistance was happening. She'd made a promise to keep Riley safe, and finding out he wasn't available didn't change that, no matter how much it stung. Robin exhaled and flung the door wide.

Clouds of gunpowder obscured the main deck, but she could see the deadly dances of men taking turns parrying and attacking. Blood smeared their faces and pooled under their feet. Blades swiped through the air with the intent to kill. Men slipped and fell and had their throats cut. Gargles and screams of anger penetrated her ears.

With that rock tumbling in her stomach, Robin stepped forward into the light. She'd never experienced anything like this, not even a gang fight. These men, so brutal and cold, reminded her of several suspects she'd detained. She shivered at the memory of the threats the suspects spat in her face when she'd cuffed them, but this was worse. So much worse, because people didn't call the police before the fights happened, and by the time emergency services arrived, all Robin found was the aftermath. Watching it happen before her eyes was paralyzing. How could men do such things to each other?

With smoke-obscured air and rapid movements, she couldn't tell who was friendly and who was foe.

To her, they were all monsters.

One man with a red bandanna wrapped over his head stabbed another, and as the body dropped to the deck, his face lit up in victory. Seeking his next target, Bandanna's eye caught on Robin. With a filthy frown on his bloody face, he used his boot to pull his sword free and kick the defeated man over.

Robin wanted to vomit, but now was not the time. His lips curled back in a sneer, displaying rotten teeth. His face was lined with age and sun damage, and his hair draped over his shoulders in knotted lengths, not that his appearance changed Robin's disgusted reaction.

Bandanna tucked away his sword and stalked closer to her as if planning on something other than a quick death. "Look what we have here. I say we found ourselves a prize worth takin.'"

"Me?" Robin backed up a step. "I'm not a prize."

Bandanna laughed. "Oh, and a feisty one at that. The men will love me for this, but you better watch that mouth of yours." His grimy hand reached out for her arm.

Robin ducked to the side and shoved the confused man forward. From behind him, she kicked the back of his left knee, and he crumpled over with a yelp. The scowling man turned on his knees.

"Why you little bi—" His angry declaration abruptly stopped, and the snicker twisting his lips slipped away, replaced by confusion.

Robin held the Glock pointed at his face, right between his ugly eyes.

"What in the bloody hell is that?"

Keeping the brute between her sights, her arms trembled. If she squeezed the trigger, a nine-millimeter bullet would fly through the man's forehead. Bandanna made no move. He'd already put away his weapon; he didn't intend to kill her. The gun shook in her hands, bouncing the sight in and out of aim.

"Some sort of toy?" Bandanna climbed to his feet and unsheathed his sword, positioning it for a strike. "I'm not afraid of toys."

Robin's vision blurred, and suddenly Mr. Coulder the bank robber appeared in her sights, aiming his gun and firing on Officer Clark Thompson. Gunshots rang in her mind, but they weren't hers. She'd only watched.

Robin flinched as her mom's panicked pleas filled her ears. The shooter had towered over her with his face shrouded in a stocking. He'd fired without a word, without a care, while Robin hid around the corner like a terrified coward with a gun in her hands, a gun loaded and ready to protect her mom. She'd broken her promise to keep mom safe.

Robin hadn't been able to take someone else's life even if it meant saving another. No wonder the force wanted her out. She couldn't handle the job. Robin's arms shook harder. Failure swept through her, and she dropped the gun with a clatter.

Bandanna's grin split wide. "As I thought. You're going to regret threatenin' me." With his sword hanging idly by his side, his meaty claw grabbed her by the nape of her neck.

Robin's lips parted in shock, and her chest squeezed in fear. There was no dispatch to radio. No partner to call on. She was on her own.

"No more funny business, or I might decide you're not a prize worth bothering for."

If she fought back, he'd kill her. If she didn't, he'd take her to his crew. Robin didn't need to guess what an angry crew capable of cold-blooded murder wanted with a woman. If those were her choices, it wasn't hard for her to lift her fists alongside her face in a boxer's stance.

If he wanted to take her, then he had to work for it.

Robin lifted her arms high and smashed his elbow downward, freeing herself. She spun away from his reach. Rolling back to her feet, she spun to find Bandanna standing still, face crumpled in pain, and Riley pulled his sword out of Bandanna's neck. Blood spurted, and his body tumbled after.

Robin collected her gun and put it back in her purse. What was the sense of keeping it if she couldn't use it against anyone? Still, it was a security blanket for her, the only normalcy in this crazy world.

"Are you injured?" Riley asked, worry creasing his brow. Stepping over the brute, Riley held out a hand, and she took it without hesitation. In the midst of all the pain and death, and no matter her opinion on his leadership decision, Riley was still her safe place until she returned home.

Riley pulled her in close and wrapped his arms around her. His warmth calmed her trembling. Over his shoulder, most of the fights were over. The deck quieted with soft groans while men picked through the carnage, checking for survivors. Since Riley was relaxed, she figured team *Angelfish* had triumphed. But she wouldn't underestimate a merchant ship again.

"I think I'm okay." Robin braced herself to be chewed out for disobeying his orders. She'd heard it all from her police captain after the Thompson shooting, from the department shrink—but in nicer words, and of course Blenny's endless reminders. All of it was unnecessary. Her nightmares were always fresh.

"This way. Let me look you over." The captain wrapped his arm around her shoulders and guided her back toward his private cabin.

Robin stared at him. "You're not mad?"

"Last I checked, I still possess all my wits," he said playfully.

Robin tilted her head in confusion.

The captain released her, sending her inside ahead of him. She expected him to close the door behind her, like a disobedient child who needed a time out, but Riley followed her, closing the door behind them both. He approached her with caution and worry.

"Are you hurt anywhere? Sometimes injuries can take time to process. I once saw a man who lost a finger and didn't realize for hours." Riley chuckled to lighten the air.

"How can you be so flippant about what happened? People died."

Dropping the levity, Riley motioned for her to sit on his bed. After she sunk into the mattress, he lifted her loose sleeves and checked her arms. "Dwelling on the darkness pulls you down farther, but when you have someone depending on you, it's easier to stay focused away from it."

He had someone depending on him, waiting on him, whoever he wrote that beautiful letter to. The woman he loved. Riley met Robin's gaze, but she looked away. Suddenly she didn't want to be this close. It was wrong. Riley lifted her pant leg next, and Robin pulled away.

"I'm fine." Changing the subject was the only way for her to pull herself from her own darkness of death, failure, and Riley's love for another. "What happened out there?"

Riley swiped his tousled hair back from his face. "The merchant ship turned out to be pirates in disguise. They hung their banner after we did. Sneaky bastards, but at least they gave us a warning. Sometimes that's the difference between walking away and being tossed overboard."

"And your crew won?" Robin asked with a twist to her face. There was no winning on the battlefield.

"If you want to count heads, we did. Randall and Karl are checking the merchant hold now. Hopefully those bloody thieves left something for the taking."

Robin shot him a look, and Riley glanced away and added, "As soon as we take whatever we need and have room for, we'll be on our way." He reached for the lower hem of her tunic. "May I check?"

"I'm fine," Robin said, pushing his hand back. "Shaken, but intact."

Riley dropped his hands. "I understand. Is there anything I can do?"

Kiss me. Hold me. Tell me it's going to be okay.

"Water would be nice."

Riley smiled and patted her thigh as he rose to his full height. "I'll be right back."

When he left, Robin stared at the diary. Why had she read it? With a groan of frustration, she fell back on the mattress. She'd sworn off men, and Riley wasn't available, so why was her heart tugging her around? This had to be some very lucid dream because time travel wasn't real.

It wasn't.

After a restless beat, Robin got off the bed. Waiting in his room within eyeshot of his diary was too much to bear. Pushing through the cabin door, Robin stared in surprise. As if the battle had never happened, the deck had been restored—cleaned, supplies at the ready, and men nonchalantly at task.

The only proof anything had happened was the merchant ship remained tied up alongside the *Angelfish*, and crew walked across a plank hauling barrels, lines, and tools on board. One man carried a small cage with chickens. Another man lifted the last dead body off the *Angelfish* deck and tossed him overboard. They weren't kidding when they'd threatened to do the same to her. Pirates were truly monsters.

Brushing that pointless opinion aside, Robin crossed the deck. While the ship was safe and the crew occupied, she might as well explore a little, distract herself. Heads turned, glaring at her, like when she'd walked the police department halls after her 'incident'.

"You don' belong here, skirt," Landry, the man with missing fingers said with a sneer.

"Aye," his partner, Kerr added. "You best be stayin' by the captain, lest something bad happens to you."

"Battle's over," Landry added. "Know what that means?"

Robin shook her head and said, "What?"

"Captain's not holding the power, so you best you be stayin' on the quartermaster's good side," Kerr said, twisting a line around a cleat.

"Gentlemen, gentlemen," a pleasant voice interrupted. Vallo approached with a smile. "Don't scare the poor thing. The captain favors her, so we should treat her with the respect a guest requires."

Robin smiled at him, grateful for the assistance.

Kerr and Landry scowled and returned to their work.

Vallo touched her arm. "With that settled, Giles is asking for you below deck."

"Thank you for your help. I don't understand why they're so upset with me."

Vallo walked her across the deck to the ladder like a bodyguard, returning hateful glances from each man they passed.

"All they know is a woman appeared on this ship, which is against the rules. They want someone to pay for the infraction. Since you wouldn't have enough money to satisfy them all, they insist on the debt being settled another way. I'm sure you can guess what that is."

Robin swallowed a thick lump. "I can."

"Fear not. If anyone's giving you grief, and the captain's not around—he's a busy man, after all—you can always come to me."

Robin smiled with appreciation blooming through her. Besides the captain, no one's been truly kind. "Thank you. I mean it."

He gestured at the ladder, and Robin waited for a turn between men carrying heavy loads. She climbed below deck with a last nod at Vallo. She didn't know why Riley warned her about him. He was great.

In the dim light, Giles the cook approached her. Riley had said he was one of the trustworthy men. She relaxed.

"There you are, Robin, is it?" Robin nodded, and he held out a mug to her. "Captain wanted me to bring you this."

"Where's Riley?" She accepted the mug and looked inside it. All she could tell in the insufficient lighting was it contained liquid.

"He's sorting a commotion in the hold. Do you peel potatoes? I could use a hand."

"Sure." Throat parched, Robin took a healthy swig and cringed. It was tart and bitter with a note of sweetness, but not nearly enough to make it palatable. She used her fist to cover her gag. After a short internal pep talk about manners and her body's need to have fluid, she swallowed and coughed. "What kind of water is this?"

"Water? We don't have water, but there's plenty of punch."

Great. Just great. Her faith in the cook's skills dramatically decreased after tasting his version of punch.

Giles gestured for her to follow him, and deeper into the belly of the ship they went. Near the stern of the ship, a stack of crates centered around a large metal pot, and a pile of raw potatoes rested on the floor. The galley. "Have a seat."

Robin lowered herself on an empty wood crate, and Giles sat next to her and resumed his peeling.

Robin picked up a potato. "Do you have an extra peeler?"

Giles cocked his round face at her. He glanced at her hands and smiled with understanding. "No knife on you? I daresay, I've got a spare somewhere." He dug in the crates behind him but came up empty. He patted his pockets and lit up when he found one. He offered her the dirty blade. "Here it is."

Had it been used to kill a guy not moments ago? Robin shivered and shook that thought away. She smiled, accepting it graciously, and set about peeling—the most normal thing she'd experienced since the festival.

"Where do you come from?" Giles asked.

"Far from here," Robin said, eyes on the spud.

Giles chuckled. "I've heard that before, like you've been coached to say it or too afraid to speak the truth. Either way, it's smart to hold back. Most of the men on this ship have never encountered a woman on board, and you can see the disruption it causes, which is why we have the rules in place. Why you chose this ship is beyond my comprehension—why any of you had, as a matter of fact. But fear not, some of us who have encountered this situation before will help you."

"What is *this* you refer to?"

She had a feeling whatever he was going to say was insulting. She braced herself.

"A woman popping out of the hold."

Well, that wasn't what she expected. "This ship is like a reverse Bermuda triangle, and I'm the next unfortunate person to take this crazy ride?"

Giles knitted his brows together in contemplation. He probably hadn't heard the concept, but he seemed to understand her point all the same. "Around these parts, you're the third so far. I don't believe in coincidence." He glanced at her with a twinkle in his eye and returned to his peeling. "I find the whole thing utterly fascinating, and I can't help but wonder if there's a young sprite out there for ol' Giles someday, but no use in wishing. I'm not the looker our previous captains have been, and I'm far from comparable to the alluring exterior of our current captain. Combine that with his big heart, and Riley's hard to resist."

Robin's brows lifted at the forward compliment.

Giles chuckled. "I daresay, I might prefer women in my bed, but I can still appreciate an attractive form when I see it, and your beauty is simply a treat to behold."

Robin's face burned with a flush of heat. "Uh, thank you."

"Pardon me, but the captain is an idiot."

Robin laughed at the unexpected statement. "What? Why would you say that?"

"Oh, that dear boy. He's been on this crew since he learned to wipe the snot off his own face. Picked 'im up fresh from a bar, straight away. He never wanted to be anything but a pirate, and although most of us never survive more than two years at sea, raiding ships, Riley's been around a long while. I've gotten to know him better than most." Giles paused.

Where was he going with this?

"He needs you."

Robin's heart skipped a beat or two. This conversation was so far removed from her expectations. "Why do you say that?"

"Has he told you about dear Gwyneth?"

Now he had her interest. "I've never heard of her. Who is she?" The woman in his diary, she'd guess. *I miss you dearly. I love you. We will be together again, soon enough.* A tight pang squeezed her chest while curiosity had her studying every movement on Giles face to glean any information possible.

"Ah. In that case. You should ask him."

Robin frowned and peeled her potato, slicing her thumb on the imperfect blade. That was like dangling a juicy bit of bacon and then eating it out of spite. It left her needing to know more.

She supposed that was the point.

Chapter 17

ROBIN HAD BEEN UNDERSTANDABLY shaken from the battle and he wanted her to relax with a refreshment. Riley wanted to be here, comforting her. Instead, he was stuck down here in the hold, dealing with the crew again. He only needed to keep them cohesive for a short while longer. Riley's tenure on this ship was coming to an end.

"She can't stay here," Kerr said. The man made a stink bigger than any other. Considering his size, it was fitting. Typically, Riley would screen men before allowing them to join the crew, but he'd detailed how urgent the recruitment was, so Randall was given power to accept any man with a working pair of hands.

Except in Landry's case of fewer digits, he had decent sailing knowledge.

Kerr had threatened Robin earlier, but even before that, Riley didn't like this man. He and his small pocket of cronies were getting on Riley's nerves. They were trying to turn the crew against him, but he couldn't formally charge any of them with anything, and tossing them overboard on no grounds would only lead to mutiny. Then both he and Robin would be in serious trouble.

"We've gone over this," Riley said, hands on his hips.

"We were interrupted," Landry countered, setting down a barrel taken from the merchant ship and standing next to his friend. Landry was a string-thin man with more sense than fingers. How he worked so efficiently with so few digits amazed Riley, honestly. But like Kerr, Riley didn't like Landry either. Fortunately, one's opinion of another didn't preclude them from working together.

"The rules state marooning is the fit punishment for stowaways. Now I agree with everyone; she gets no exception no matter who she is, *but...*" Landry trailed off to capture the attention of those around him.

Riley was certainly listening.

"But the nearest suitable island is too far from our course. We'd lose too much time. Instead, I have a satisfactory substitute, and it's one you can't deny."

Substitute meant she'd be stranded somewhere else. Riley's jaw tightened.

"With an empty ship over the rail, we can send her over and cut her free. Problem solved," Landry said with a self-satisfied smirk.

Over Riley's dead body would he allow these animals to abandon Robin, leaving her to fend for herself on the empty merchant ship and die of dehydration or starvation, while these men sailed away to their own riches. "She's staying on *this* ship until I disembark myself. I expect coordinated thievery from you, but that's cruel and you know it."

"That's funny coming from you." Kerr leaned in close as if trying to intimidate Riley into submission.

Riley restrained himself from punching the man in his plump face. Instead, Riley leaned forward, meeting his challenge. "What's that supposed to mean?"

"Word buzzing around says you insisted on marooning the last woman on this ship. You yourself led the charge against her, but now you changed your tune. Imagine that."

Riley had been the voice of the crew under Captain Henry Price. Like the situation at hand, Riley's duty then had been to stand against the captain in the matters of Miss Angela. Personally, he didn't like a woman on board. She was too disruptive. Was then and continued to be now.

But Captain Price had found a way, and Riley would, too.

"Even better, I think the wench needs a companion on the empty ship," Green, another new man, added with a petulant tone and stared Riley in the eye. "Someone who understands her. Someone to rescue her from a slow suffering death."

Green implied Riley was going to join her on the merchant ship, so he could kill her, saving her from dying a miserable death like a pirate. The idea of Riley being forced into something so heinous angered him to no end, and he couldn't sail the ship with only one unexperienced sailor. Riley grit his teeth and squeezed his fists. Their escalation was getting out of control.

"Are you suggesting a mutiny?" Riley asked, body rigid for a fight.

"Now, now, men. We can discuss this calmly," Vallo said with a friendly tone, inserting himself between Riley and Green.

Riley sent Vallo a suspicious brow. He, of all men, was the least trusted. If Riley had it his way, the traitor would've been cast overboard with the bodies from the battle.

"The only thing keepin' us calm is following the rules," Kerr replied while glaring at Riley. "Until someone steps up and decides to lead based on our written agreement, I consider us in a pickle."

"Well, for one I agree with the captain," Vallo said, sending him a friendly smile. "Let the woman stay with us. She's not the first. Possibly not the last. What harm is there in allowing her to help? We're all strong men, capable of containing our whimsies, capable of *patience*. Our turn will come."

Riley didn't like that last statement, but for now he needed to ignore it. With a liked crew member in agreement with him, Riley sent an appreciative, if not apprehensive, glance at Vallo. Now was his chance to redirect the crew before things got too far out of hand to rein in. "Vallo's right. Do we have the guns and enough shot to make a noise at the fort?"

McKee, said, "Sufficient shot for all hands. Plenty of swords and pistols, too. I'll make sure they're cleaned and prepared, but in this matter, there is no concern."

"Good. Now if we're done here, I have things to do." Riley turned on his heels.

"Better not be with that skirt," Landry warned.

"By rights, we deserve our turn with her," Kerr added. Snickers bounced around the tight room. "I'm glad Randall ordered her to her sleep down below with the crew. Who knows what will happen?"

Riley couldn't believe what he heard. "Robin is not to be touched. End of discussion." Riley moved his hand to the hilt of his cutlass. "Anyone unclear?"

The men stayed silent, biding their time. When Riley decided on Fort James as the target, he'd planned on rewarding his crew with treasure beyond belief and with his own sacrifice, making sure the crew survived to spend it. A worthy end to a long piratical career. But their lack of appreciation for his efforts had him doubting his plan.

Riley met the angry gazes from several of the crew, but they dared not speak up. They were placated for the moment, but it wouldn't last. Riley had to do something more, but even if it worked, he could never trust these men.

Robin had claimed the future was safe, despite Riley's firsthand experience, and every moment on this ship was a risk to her life. These men were animals. Riley needed to get her home before it was too late.

With a warning glare, Riley took his leave and found his quartermaster on the upper deck discussing logistics with Boatswain Karl. The captain had no time to waste with the threats to Robin's life.

"Randall, might I have a word?"

"Excuse me a minute, Karl," the quartermaster said, and Karl left. Out of earshot, Randall asked, "What is it, captain?"

"Kerr and Landry are threatening to leave Robin on the merchant ship when we set sail. I need you to get them under control before we reach the Gambia. That river has no exit points. We're either all in or not at all, and there's no room for disagreements."

Randall crossed his arms over his chest. "You put me in a quandary of a position. You're asking those men to ignore a grievous disregard for the rules that holds this crew in one piece...in order for the crew to function as one piece? That doesn't make sense. The solution to your problem was already given. Relieve the crew of the woman or share her.

I've sailed on many ships, and never has this been a point of contention."

Riley's hand squeezed the hilt at his side. "Two shares of the prize for each man. Three for the officers."

Randall's brows lifted. "A rate simply unheard of. If what you say about Fort James is accurate, that is a substantial offer. You must love that woman."

Riley flinched. Why would the quartermaster make such an assumption? He was only doing right by protecting an innocent woman. Ignoring the ridiculous accusation, Riley said, "Do we have an accord then?"

"This raid was your idea. What about your share?"

Where Riley was going, he didn't need anything. "None."

Randall backed up a step, lips parting.

"But I insist Robin receives a share in my stead." Just in case things didn't go as planned.

Randall's lips pressed for a moment. "I'll convey the offer and do my best to insist their acceptance."

"Thank you." Riley patted the man's shoulder and set off.

He'd dampened the fire on their intent to abandon Robin or steal her for their own amusement, but at any moment the crew could mutiny, leaving Riley's efforts void. And now Randall's words had him fretting. Since meeting Robin in the future, weeks of drunkenness proved he couldn't get her out of his head, but the recent threats to her life showed him something he hadn't felt in a long time.

He needed to protect her—not to clear his conscious before the final raid, but because he, in fact, loved her.

18

Chapter 18

Despite the primitive toilet in the captain's private quarters opening directly into the ocean, the noise and stomach upset from sleeping in a swinging hammock with the crew, horrible food, and almost undrinkable...*punch*, Robin managed to crack a smile. She didn't know what had changed, but the men were ignoring her, rather than looking at her as an enemy or a piece of meat.

She sipped from her mug what Riley had said was ale, and her face pinched, reminding her of learning to acquire the taste for beer at twenty-three years old. The more she exposed herself to the tart flavor, the better it would get. At least, that was what she told herself with every swallow, and it was still better than the punch.

She'd once thought going back in time would be a fun vacation. That was the dumbest thought she'd ever had.

William Price, the lanky armorer, stood at the head of the mess hall and lifted a mug for a toast. He called out for everyone's attention, and he hiccupped. When the crew quieted down, he said, "Many of you never met Hyde, our night watch on the *Sea Lion*. The man never cracked a smile in all my years of knowing him. Except once."

Men who knew the story chuckled with their memories. Price nodded to them with a wide, knowing grin.

"We had taken the *Elizabeth*, and Hyde wanted only one prize. He darted for the captain's private stash, claiming he could sniff out top-shelf wine like a dog. While we inventoried the hold and cleared out everything of value, Hyde found the captain's stash all right."

More chuckles followed and Price grinned.

"While we watched, he drank down his prize as if proving his prowess, but not a second later he spit it out in a fit of disgust. Turned out the captain kept empty bottles around for the times he couldn't make it to the head." Price folded over in his own drunken laughter.

Fits erupted throughout the hall. Liquid splashed from mugs, and men began singing in the far corner, which rapidly spread through the hall. A violin joined the tempo. Robin couldn't help a smile at their cheerfulness, so different from what she'd seen before.

A hand settled on Robin's shoulder, and a whisper tickled her ear. "Do you want to get out of here?"

Robin's lips pulled into a smile, and she tilted her head to find Captain Riley, but the smile slid away. A hint of despair shadowed his handsome features. What could be wrong? She took his offered hand. "Yes, please."

The captain gripped her tightly as he led her away from the wild after-dinner noise. Robin caught disapproving looks from Kerr and Landry on the way, and a shiver of nerves tore through her. At least they didn't say anything.

Up the ladder, Robin stood with Riley under a blanket of stars. Gentle waves lapped at the hull, and a soft breeze fluttered her hair. The music wafted up from below deck, a spirited violin accompanied by happy voices.

With a note of seriousness on his brow, Riley turned to her and said, "After all you've been through, you deserve far better from me, from all this." He waved his arms around to indicate the ship.

Robin frowned. Where was he going with this?

"Please hear me out. I have a favor to ask of you, and I want you to consider it carefully. But I'll give you my disclaimer first, I don't want you do to it."

Robin's lips lifted, disbelieving the severity of this mysterious request. "You can't give me all that lead up and not tell me what it is."

Riley ran a hand down his face, distraught.

Okay, now Robin was getting nervous. What did the captain want her to do that he didn't want her to? With the looks she'd received on her way up from below deck, she imagined the worst.

"Does...does this have to do with the crew's hate for me? Do you need me to"—she could hardly finish the sentence—"*placate* Kerr, Landry, and Green?"

"No, oh, no, not at all. Never. Don't ever think you would have to do something like that. I would never allow it." Riley collected her hands in his. "I sent a letter ahead to Commander Mitchell of Fort James, requesting an audience to discuss business. He regretfully declined, so I needed something more persuasive. I replied with an insistence my wife wanted to see the protection the commander offered the English Crown, and that she was especially impressed with the guns I'd told her about and the vast supply of soldiers."

The part of his story that stuck in her mind and replayed like a broken record was 'my wife'. The beautiful letter in the diary was to his *wife*. Robin couldn't believe after all this the man was actually taken, confirming what she'd dreaded. Robin didn't know whether to be insulted at his flirtatious behavior or hate herself for allowing herself to care so much.

"The commander accepted. You see my problem?"

What did any of this have to do with her? She looked at his hands holding hers. "Your wife's not here."

"Precisely. I need you to pose as my wife."

"What if I wasn't here?"

"Then I'd be putting a wig and dress on Buckley. Our odds would be ever slimmer." Captain attempted a humorous smile, but it didn't touch his eyes.

Riley needed her to pretend for this commander guy, but he didn't *want* her to do it. Did Robin remind Riley of his wife too much? Was she a temporary substitute until they got back together?

Not days ago, he kissed her like it was his last time. The vibes from him were clear that he had feelings for her, but this simple act of pretend was too much for him? Did he think of Gwyneth when he'd kissed Robin? She checked her anger and asked evenly, "Why don't you want me to do it?"

Riley exhaled. "It's dangerous."

"You said you handled the crew."

"Nothing is a guarantee, but it's not that."

"I don't understand." Robin freed her hands and folded her arms over her chest, hugging herself. "What did you do that being close to you is so dangerous?"

Riley flinched as if her words stung. "It's not what I've done, but what I will do."

"And that is?"

Riley sat on the rail and stuffed a hand through his hair. There was so much he wasn't telling her.

"What's already been set in motion cannot be undone. For that, I am sorry. Your cooperation, I believe, will help us succeed in my plan for the crew, but having you join me puts your life at great risk. One that pained me greatly to ask of you."

Robin stared, still waiting for him to give her something to understand.

After a pause, Riley's burdened face met hers. "If I leave you behind with the crew, our odds of success are far too slim, and I've told you about the narrow string keeping the crew in line. So you see, I must leave you behind, but yet I cannot. The risk is yours to decide. Pretend to be my wife when we pose as merchants at Fort James or stay on the ship with the crew. Kerr, Landry, and Green will be remaining on the ship during the meeting."

Since the crew still harbored resentment toward her, the answer was easy. Robin approached him. "I'll go with you to the fort, but I don't see how it's dangerous."

"Then I have failed to properly convey the situation. Fort James rests on a spit of land in the center of a river with cliffs, impassable mangroves, and sand dunes on either side. It has reinforced stone walls, harbors dozens of trained and armed soldiers at the ready with access to an endless armory, all led by an esteemed English commander. It is nigh impenetrable, and escape depends on...luck."

"Wait." Robin held up one hand while pressing the other against her forehead. "You want to stroll in there acting as merchants and overpower all the soldiers inside?"

"That is precisely correct."

"Why?" Robin could guess, since they were pirates and all, but she wanted him to say it.

"What do you think all that protects?"

"The English Crown?" she repeated his phrase.

"A vault of immeasurable wealth."

Figures. Robin couldn't even be upset about it, but the risk was beginning to settle into her mind, along with doubt.

"You think this crew can outmatch trained soldiers with weapons...and all their fingers?"

"I must be transparent with you before you confirm your decision."

Robin sat on the rail next to him, her thighs touching his.

"I hadn't planned on leaving the fort," he said softly, like it was a secret confession.

"What do you mean, like taking it over as commander?"

Since the crew had been on the verge of mutiny, that didn't seem like a bad plan.

"No." Riley stared at the deck, too ashamed to look her in the eye.

Not leaving the fort, but not taking over... He didn't mean, no, he couldn't choose something so selfish as that. Realization sunk in like a rock headed straight to her gut. Riley had nearly begged her to take him to the authorities. He didn't need to atone for a crime committed, no. Guilt of some sort drove him to want to end his suffering.

Robin appreciated he admitted his troubles to her, but she was furious he'd concoct a plan like that in the first place. It wasn't her place to be angry at him, but she couldn't stop it from punctuating her words. She hopped down off the rail and faced him. "This wasn't about *risk*. You wanted the crew to steal their riches, and you were going to sacrifice yourself so they could escape."

Riley nodded, confirming her theory. He still wouldn't meet her eye.

How could he do that? It was so selfish she wanted to slap him. "You *wanted* to kill yourself."

A glimmer of light reflected off the tears on his cheeks. Robin's heart broke for him. He was hurting still, and the anger drained away.

"Please don't think lesser of me. If I could go back and dash this plan from my head, I would. But it's too late now." He lifted his face her.

Robin reached out and wiped his tears away.

Riley pulled back.

Robin reached out again and closed her hands over his. Regardless of what his wife would think, Robin was going through with the plan to make sure Riley made it home to her. Gwyneth would have to forgive Riley's faults, or she wouldn't get him back at all. "If we are to pretend to be married, we need to be comfortable with one another. Let me do what I do best."

"What's that?"

"I'll cover your back, as long as you have mine." Good thing she brought her Glock.

Fresh tears glistening, Riley's lips pulled into a small smile. "I want to celebrate your agreement, but I admit I'm afraid. For tonight, dance with me." Riley hopped off the rail and framed his arms in invitation.

Robin glanced over her shoulders. "Does the crew know about this?"

Riley chuckled. "Their ire remains, but their disagreement has been settled. Join me."

"But that was for me to stay here, alive, not this—"

Riley pressed a finger against her lips and hushed her.

With a smile, Robin stepped into his arms, and his hands enveloped her. He moved them around the deck, slower than the melody commanded and careful to avoid obstacles in their path. A man overhead in the crow's nest sang a tune accompanying the music from below deck. Riley and Robin looked up and laughed.

And at once, Riley sang along.

Robin lost herself in his beautiful baritone melody, not listening to the words, but absorbing the fluid sounds comforting her. He carried them around the deck, avoiding obstacles, her and him, the sea, and the moon. And the beautiful music. And her heart sang. Despite knowing better, despite her history with getting involved with those too close to her, Robin's heart lifted with the melody.

Riley pressed against her and whispered into her ear, "You shouldn't have come here, but I'm grateful you did. Kiss me."

Before Robin could consider how she'd ended up in the past, his request brought their previous kiss to mind, and Robin wanted nothing else.

Riley leaned down, giving her easy reach to his lips, and he stopped their dance.

Robin gripped him tight. Heat surged through her body, pooling and throbbing down low, and she brought her lips to his. They were warm, soft, with little scratches of his grown-in beard. He pressed into her harder, and while they changed positions, she focused on his hips. To feel if he wanted her as much as she wanted him. She was going to keep kissing him until she felt him.

She hadn't forgiven his decision to take on the merchant ship, but to her, the captain had been kind and generous. He was a fabulous dancer with the voice of an angel. He was absolutely nothing like Blenny, or Angry Boston, or Riggs.

A strike of jealousy rushed through her.

Forgive us, Gwyneth.

RILEY HATED SHOWING HIS tears to her, but she moved him in ways he didn't know possible. He gripped the stunning woman from the future tightly, like his life depended on it, because it did. He didn't want to let her go, but he had to...eventually. That was a painful thought for another time.

He was a selfish bastard for asking her to take a chance for his unruly crew and his meaningless existence, but she agreed anyway—knowing full well the circumstances and risk involved. Now that she'd made her choice, it was up to him to keep her safely at his side, because he couldn't live with himself if something happened to her. The thin connection between them was the only thing keeping Riley's head level. He made many mistakes in his years on the sea, including taking the pirate ship disguised as Spanish merchants, but finding Robin might've been one right thing.

If they survived.

Captain Riley released her lips and hugged her tight, rocking with the music. Bauer, up in the mast, continued a gentle tune for them. The violin below deck quieted as the crew crashed for the night. Such as they must. Tomorrow they'd disembark and meet their fate. Tonight was too short.

Pulling back, he said, "Join me in my cabin tonight."

Robin's plumped lips parted. "We can't do that. The crew—"

"The crew is going to be wired and anxious over tomorrow's raid. You won't get any rest next to them."

Her lips twisted into a half-smile. "Who says I'd get any rest sharing your bed?"

Riley's head fell back, and he groaned at her forwardness. How did he get so lucky to meet a woman like her?

Robin's hands reached around his neck and pulled him back down to this new, amazing reality. "Let's go."

Riley grasped her hand in his and led her to his cabin. They slipped behind the door. Only the night watchman would've seen, but since Bauer offered the serenade, he mustn't mind.

Robin stopped in the middle of the dimly lit room. Moonlight bathed the floor in an aqua color, and Riley lit a candle. He wanted to see her. All of her.

He removed his bandolier with weapons and stalked up to her. Her eyes were hot, waiting for him. Not one to leave a lady wanting, his lips came down on hers once again, and he reached for her hips, sliding her dress up and exposing her smooth middle. She wore modern undergarments, and they were...quite pleasing.

His cock strained his breeches, and Robin panted, heaving her chest in the most alluring way.

She backed up a step, arms moving to wrap around her exposed middle. "This feels like some fairytale, but it's real. This is real, isn't it?"

"As real as my touch."

Thoughts wrestling in her mind displayed on her face. Robin sighed and frowned. She backed up another step and gestured to his bed. "I can't do this. You know I can't. I'm sorry. I thought I could." She picked up the dress.

With desperation and frustration coursing through him, he reminded himself he might not be a gentleman, but Robin was a lady. "Pardon my forwardness. It was not my intention to offend."

Robin pushed the dress over her head and wouldn't meet his eyes. "I have to go. Yeah, I have to. Goodnight."

And just like that, she vanished.

What the hell did he do wrong?

Chapter 19

ROBIN AWOKE IN THE swaying hammock with a headache and a dull pain in her shoulder. Carrying the weight of her gun and spare mags in her purse for so long was draining, and once again, she didn't catch enough sleep. The snores were one thing, pretending to be Riley's wife while he was already happily married was another. Robin needed to go home, she wanted to, so why was the pretend situation so upsetting?

With a groan, Robin fumbled her legs free of the loose fabric and sat up. The hammocks around her were empty, but an extra-large shadow of a man stood over her. Robin gasped.

"As payment for your passage, I have a need for you to satisfy. It's lodged somewhere here in my breeches." Kerr gripped her arm and forced her hand on his crotch.

Suddenly wide awake and completely disgusted, Robin twisted out of his grip and rolled backward across the hammock and up to her feet.

"What the...?" Kerr said with a growl. "Get back here."

"Keep your hands off me," she demanded. Knowing how precarious her presence was, provoking the man was a bad idea, but after that move, she felt it necessary. "You pig."

Kerr growled and shifted his weight to grab her, but Robin rushed through the gun deck filled with swaying hammocks, and climbed to the main deck. The crew was huddled around the captain's door. By the angry tones, something was wrong. Had something happened to Riley?

Heart pounding, Robin found a path to weave her way through the crowd while listening, hoping for safety in numbers and a distraction keeping her safe from Kerr.

"We never agreed to this. If you get a woman in your bed, then we all do."

Hollers of agreement startled Robin.

She checked her purse, verifying her Glock was still there, before slinging it in front of her body for easy access. Robin approached the captain's doorway, and through the stench, she found Riley filling the space, shirtless and terribly distracting. But alive.

"Now we get to tell her to her face," Landry said with a sneer.

Robin turned to face the missing-fingered man, and Riley shot her a quick look of apology before addressing the brute.

"Landry, have you spoken to the night watchman?" Riley shot a glare at Randall, who stood by the angry crew and wasn't doing his job of controlling them. "He can corroborate the amount of time Robin and I spent together. It's been a while since you were my age, but I assure you, I need more than a few moments with a woman."

A few men chuckled. The rest stared at him like they wanted him dead. If all these men had the quartermaster looking out for their own interests, who protected Riley?

Kerr approached from the back and glared at Robin. "We acquiesced to leavin' her on this ship and keepin' our hands off her for a hefty price. A price based on promises that have yet to be fulfilled. Her warmin' your bed wasn't part of the deal. She has to warm ours, too."

More angry hollers of agreement. A tingle of nerves skittered along her flesh, and the hairs on her arms lifted.

Muscles rippled beneath Riley's skin as anger erupted in his own sharp voice. "She is the only person on this ship that can guarantee your prize. Listen up, everyone. I did promise you double the normal share on this account, but for you to get that share, we need Robin, and you need me. From this point forward, Robin is to be treated, not as a woman, not as a lesser, not as an object, but as one of the crew. And until we reach the shore of Gambia Island, she will share my bed, and *only* my bed. If anyone has a problem with that, challenge me now."

Robin gaped at him. If he wanted to incite a mutiny, she figured that was an efficient way.

"Any settling of disagreements is done on land, captain," Randall said evenly. "That's also in the articles."

Riley leaned into the older man's face. "This time I'm breaking the rules on purpose, so the men can return to what's important. Doesn't seem like anyone wants to focus on our account here."

"Randall," Kerr said, touching the man's arm with a light air of confidence. "The winner takes over as captain until the next vote. I think my skills would be a perfect fit."

Riley tensed. "Are you directly challenging me, Kerr?"

The man stood a few inches taller than Riley, but he tilted his thick chin up to make his point. "You heard me."

This couldn't be happening. Taken or not, Robin couldn't let Gwyneth become a widow when Robin could do something about it. She tugged on Riley's forearm, pulling him back a step, and she shifted her body in front of him as a shield. Robin two-handed her Glock and aimed at the angry crowd. "Back off. As the captain said, we have more important things to focus on."

The men exchanged glances of confusion and a couple chuckled.

Kerr belly laughed. "What are you going to do with that? Bop me on the head with it?"

The crew roared with laughter.

Robin's finger moved to the trigger. Demanding a favor in exchange for payment owed hardly justified a man's death no matter how depraved the favor to Robin was. Robin unwittingly broke their rules. They were right to be upset. Her vision slipped into a blur. Her hands trembled, bouncing her sight all over. Robin couldn't do it. She couldn't pull the trigger to defend herself. What was wrong with her? How was she going to protect Riley if she couldn't protect herself against a pig who deserved it? Robin's pulse pounded in her ears, and her chest rose and fell with growing panic.

Blenny had been right. Something was wrong with her.

Captain Riley's hand gently pushed the barrel down. He whispered into her ears, softening the pounding panic. "I have to do this."

"They're going to kill you," she whispered back, remembering his suicidal ideations. "I won't let that happen."

Riley's lips lifted in amusement. "Have you so little faith in my skills?"

Robin's mouth opened and closed, unable to answer that. She hadn't seen him fight, besides his wild attempt on a car bumper, but he'd also told her he wanted to end it all. Did she trust his word that he'd changed his mind? He seemed too quick to accept a mortal fight.

"Main deck in ten minutes," Riley said to his challenger. His voice rose, "Clear the deck. Prepare for a duel."

Kerr nodded and set off to prepare. Men dispersed to move barrels, lines, and stray supplies aside. Riley gestured with his head to invite her inside. She swept in quickly, and Riley closed the cabin door behind them. Without addressing the situation, he shifted through the clothes on the floor for his tunic.

"Are you crazy?" Robin spun on him.

Riley lifted a tunic and pulled it over his head. "If you would've asked me a few weeks ago, I would've said yes."

His nonchalance for the situation frustrated her. "They mean to kill you."

He tucked the tunic into his breeches. "It's a rare thing to have a captain unchallenged. It takes a great feat of bravery to do it in front of everyone. The crew needs a leader. They need someone to tell them what to do and in exchange, they're rewarded for it. Kerr is not a follower, and he's forward enough to vocalize it. The only unexpected part of this is the unfortunate timing. Rather than waiting until landfall, which is customary, we must settle this now. Where we're going, there won't be time for a duel."

Robin frowned, hating that a fight to the death was so commonplace and not in the least troubling to him. "Tell me you aren't going to lose."

Captain Riley's hands stilled, and he met her gaze. Riley laced his fingers through hers, and at the warm sensation, she closed her eyes, steeling herself for the answer she didn't want.

"I don't know what happened last night between us. We must speak of it later. But since you are comfortable with my touch, we'll have no trouble taking the fort."

Robin held his eyes again. "And if we never reach the fort?"

Riley shook his head with a smile. "Use that strange weapon you keep aiming. It does something effective, does it not?"

Robin frowned.

"I only jest," Riley said with a small lift of his lips. "I've sailed the seas for nearly a decade. I've been in this same situation plenty of times."

"You were challenged for the captaincy before?"

Riley released her hands and lifted his weapon belt. He wrapped around his waist and hung it over a shoulder. "I've taken men's lives with a blade several times before."

Robin dropped her eyes. Self-defense was one thing, and Robin believed in second chances, but *several*? Deadpan, she said, "You're a pirate. I shouldn't have expected anything different. Both of you can go slaughter a man who doesn't agree with you. See what that solves."

She turned to leave, but Riley's hand rested on her shoulder. With a sigh, she faced him.

Desperation filled his face. "Please be assured it was never without reason. Most of us don't want to take lives, but sometimes an amicable solution cannot be found otherwise. Kerr instigated this, and if I decline to follow through, they'll take the ship, and you and I..." he trailed off, voice breaking. Taking a moment to compose himself, he added, "They don't take kindly to cowardice."

Robin pulled away, hating the situation. "They mean to kill you."

"I didn't expect anyone to call my bluff this close to a historic raid, but for your sake, I cannot ignore the challenge. So long as you remain aboard, I cannot allow them to take control. The choice is no longer in my hands." He leaned in close, breath warming her face. "Unless that black thing you wave around is some magic force from the future, my sword is all that stands between them and you."

He was right. The crew had backed him into a corner on this. Riley had to fight. His steely gray eyes met her worried gaze, and his lips came down to hers. Her arms wrapped around his upper back and his hands pressed her lower back closer. She could never get close enough. She kissed him like it was a goodbye kiss, because as much as she wanted to believe his words, Robin wasn't so sure a large, angry man with dozens of supporters could defeat a resigned one.

As their lips shifted, Robin realized he could be thinking of his wife Gwyneth. If so, Robin could grant a man that last wish. Robin couldn't heed her own rule about dating colleagues, so her heart would be crushed, regardless. Perhaps his could be healed still.

The captain pulled away too soon and hesitated at the door. "I have full confidence in my abilities, but if for some unbelievable reason I don't win, I want you to know I'm sorry."

"For what?" Robin gripped the strap of her purse, fearing the answer.

The corner of Riley's lips lifted in a sad smile, and he left, swallowed by the crowd pumped full of anticipation.

Robin didn't want to wait here, while he was out there, defending them. But she couldn't face his death. The strap of her purse slipped, and Robin repositioned it. She had her Glock.

Chapter 20

THE CROWD WATCHED INTENTLY as Captain Riley and his challenger circled, swords in hand. Riley's feet were sure and steady, his hands tight and ready. Kerr was a bigger man with a longer reach, but he was also older. Riley had years of experience, youth, and quickness on his side. Riley also had something Kerr didn't: A woman who cared.

And she happened to be watching.

Riley wasn't trying to impress her with his swordsmanship. He only wanted to dispatch the challenger and return to the plan, with Robin safely by his side. If the outcome should be unfavorable, the crew would destroy her self-worth, abuse her in ways he couldn't stomach, and rip her to pieces for spite. Riley skimmed the crew, searching for her, but she no longer stood where she had been. Riley tore his eyes back to his competitor. Whatever might've been happening to her now was nothing compared to what would happen if Riley fell to the sword.

"Gonna circle all afternoon, captain?" Kerr taunted.

Riley had been waiting for Kerr to make the first move. At the larger man's insistence, Riley struck.

Kerr parried easily.

Another strike and parry combination. Then Riley waited, wanting Kerr to begin his attack.

"Come on, captain. I don't have all day. There's a woman waiting for me." Kerr sneered.

Gritting his jaw, Riley swiped fast and dodged a return swing, anger driving his movements. With another strike, he sliced the man on the forearm, but it wasn't enough.

Kerr touched the wound and laughed. "Little man makes little cuts."

A few observers chortled softly. The rest were too enthralled in the fight to react to Kerr's baseless insult. Kerr had never seen Riley fight. It was brave but stupid to challenge an unknown opponent with such high stakes. Some lessons were only learned once.

Riley gestured to strike again, but he held back, forcing Kerr to move. Riley countered his opponent's shift and struck him on the hip.

Kerr wasn't laughing any longer.

The crowd murmured. No one braved to cheer. Showing loyalties to either meant instant problems for the victor. Riley was fine with that. The fewer distractions, the better. His eyes returned to the crew, seeking Robin.

With his eyes averted from the fight, Riley had no time to parry a striking blade. He leaned back as the blade pierced his shoulder.

Kerr laughed.

Riley stumbled backward and leaned against the cabin wall. He touched the searing wound, and blood soaked his fingers. His lips parted. He couldn't lose. He had no intention of losing. But the slickness on his fingers and poor range of motion didn't bode well.

WORRY LINES FORMED ON Riley's brow as his fingers pulled back with blood. Robin gasped, straining on her tippytoes. How bad was the wound? Could he still fight? Fury roared deep in her chest. These monsters stood around watching like this was some sport, but too chicken to stop them. Too unreasonable to accept a calm discussion. Too barbaric.

All of them were monsters.

Except Riley.

Robin wasn't going to watch him get killed because she somehow appeared on his ship. Robin gripped the Glock firmly in her hand and wove through the crowd, fighting their bulk and unreasonable stench. When she found the man with a raised sword about to kill Riley, Robin palmed her weapon with both hands. Her finger shifted to the trigger. She lined up her shot. Kerr's head was angled and protected by his arms. She shifted the barrel to the man's chest.

Shoot him.

Do it now!

Her vision blurred. Her hands shook. Not again! She simply needed to squeeze, take his life, the life of a man who hadn't done anything wrong besides argue about some frivolous rules they'd all agreed to and made her touch him. She didn't know Kerr personally. Was he a terrible man? Had he done awful things? Most importantly, was he right to insist on following the rules they'd agreed to?

Robin tried to steady her arms and focus the shaky sight. With the added rocking of the ship and her unsteady balance, she couldn't line up the shot. Her hands wouldn't let her take a man's life, even if that meant saving another.

What the hell was wrong with her?

Kerr's blade came down, and Robin screamed with her eyes closed and squeezed the trigger. A stupid, stupid move, but it was too late to do it over.

Her chest rose and fell, but she dared not look at what she'd done. Someone grabbed her shoulder and shook. Robin tucked the gun into her purse and covered her face in her hands. The men would be very angry with her. For interfering. For killing a man—one of their men.

"Robin," a man's voice said.

On a sigh, she moved aside her trembling hands. The cook stood before her, lips pressed firmly. The other men around her had moved away, giving her and Giles space.

"What have I done?" she whispered, knees shaking. "I'm sorry. I couldn't stand by and do nothing."

"Go help the captain." Giles said gently.

Robin tilted her head in misunderstanding, and the cook moved aside. Both combatants sprawled on the deck, blood spilled.

Tears shimmied her vision, and she stumbled over, knees giving way. She watched the rise and fall of Riley's chest. Shallow. The captain's hand moved, and with great effort he sat upright, breathing hard with pain. His eyes locked on hers.

"Are you okay? Stupid question. So stupid. I'm sorry."

Riley chuckled and grunted from the effort. The sound was wet. "That's to be determined."

"What did I do?" Robin glanced at the fallen opponent, still lifeless.

"You startled everyone. That's what you did." Riley sent her a crooked smile and closed one eye against the blood running down his forehead. "That magic weapon of yours sure has a kick."

Robin gripped the captain around the waist and helped him to his feet. "Am I in trouble? Are they going to...?" she trailed off, afraid of the consequences.

"Don't concern yourself. I think they're puzzled by that gun of yours. It's not a toy after all."

A pair of men rushed to Kerr's body and rolled him over. With morbid curiosity, she scanned his body for evidence of a bullet hole, but there wasn't one. "Didn't I hit him?"

Riley glanced over his injured shoulder with a wince and said, "Not unless you struck him with a steel blade."

"I didn't kill him?" Robin asked pointlessly, voice raised in relief.

"No." Riley turned to the spectators and said, "Get back to work, men. We have a fort to raid."

Men moved into action, keeping quiet. Three men hoisted Kerr off the deck and tipped him overboard.

Robin gasped. "Are they throwing him over?"

"If he were a respected man of honor, he'd be wrapped in his hammock and given a proper ceremony. Since he isn't, what else are we going to do with him?" Riley leaned in close to her ear and whispered, "You don't eat people in the future do you? I thought your food tasted strange."

Robin stared at him, mouth gaped in complete disbelief. Riley winked at her, but she couldn't process that he'd made a joke.

"Let's go to my cabin. I need clean clothes," Riley said, lifting the hem of his shredded and bloody shirt.

Robin assisted his steps. One man, on his hands and knees, scrubbed the puddle off the deck. With a cringe, Robin brought Riley into the captain's private cabin and closed the door. She released him on the mattress and kneeled at his trunk of clothes. "You bandolier should have leather straps on both shoulders. Would've saved you some damage."

Riley didn't answer. He slowly peeled off his weapon holster.

Robin shifted through his private belongings. Deep under the layers, where she hadn't ventured during the hunt for her own attire, she found a small sketch of a young couple. Robin squinted at it. The man had a striking resemblance to Riley, who winced removing his tunic. And the woman…that must be Gwyneth. Pressure squeezed her chest. A lucky woman was waiting for him. Jealousy ripped through her. She wanted Riley. For once in her life, she wanted a man, but he was taken. Politely, she said, "She's beautiful."

Riley dropped his tunic on the floor. "Yes."

"Gwyneth is a lucky woman," Robin said wistfully. It wasn't entirely appropriate, but she had to say what she felt. If he hated her forward implication, she'd apologize, but she didn't want to.

Riley raked a hand through his disheveled and tangled hair, fingers catching. He blew out a deep sigh of pain. "Word always gets around. The men on this ship gossip like a group of women at tea. What did they tell you?"

"They didn't tell me anything." Robin took in his chiseled bare chest smeared with dirt and blood. Heat rose in her cheeks. Underneath the grime, which she'd had the pleasure of seeing in her apartment, he was a beautiful man. With the grime, his strength was plain sexy.

And that only made her feel worse.

Riley stared at her with disbelief on his features. "After what they did to you, I'm surprised you're protecting them."

"I'm not," Robin insisted. "Giles told me her name. Nothing more." After a short pause, Robin had to know more. She pressed, "Is she waiting for you back home?"

Riley lifted himself off the mattress high enough to pull his breeches down. With his injured shoulder, he only used one arm. Robin should've helped, but she didn't want to push too far into his comfort zone. She should've looked away but forget it. He wasn't bashful, and neither was she.

"My father insisted I accept a marriage proposal from the neighboring landowner. It was a good match for our poor family. Of all the available suitors, I have no idea why I was chosen."

"I could guess," Robin interrupted with a shy smile.

Riley shot her a confused look, but continued while sitting back down, "I agreed before I met her. When she arrived down from her home in her carriage, sporting an ocean's worth of material in her dress, and her nose pinched in the air against our farm smells, I knew life would never be the same."

Riley shook the breeches off his feet, leaving him in socks and some antique form of underwear in a beige color. It wasn't flattering, but he could've been wearing a windbreaker from the nineteen-nineties and still been hot.

"Do you want a hand with that?" she asked.

"I've had worse." Riley shook a long lock out of his face and winced. The corner of his lips lifted as if hiding how much pain he was suffering. "Shortly after the agreement had been settled, my father passed away. I didn't want to stay, and it took little to convince Gwyneth to make a new life in the colonies away from the filth. Her brother sailed with us across the Atlantic on a slaver." He stopped abruptly, before his voice cracked.

The story was upsetting him, and it was none of her business, anyway. "I'm sorry for pushing."

Riley collected her hands and motioned for her to sit next to him, so she did, carefully.

"During the voyage, they both caught the fevers. With her last breaths, Gwyneth cursed me and my father and regretted the trip. She wished she'd never met me." Riley's head fell in shame.

Robin squeezed his hands. "Their deaths were not your fault."

Riley lifted a brow. "Easier said than believed, am I correct?"

Robin's face burned hot. Without a word, she nodded.

Riley continued his story. "When I arrived at port, I buried them both. With nothing left to live for, I took to the seas, raiding and pillaging ships, hoping for the glory of the win and the finality of the end. That's the truth, and now you know the real me. And if you hate the animal I've become, I understand."

Robin glanced at the floor and rubbed her thumbs on his knuckles. "I don't think you're an animal at all. You're the kindest man I've ever met, believe it or not. And I'm so sorry for your losses. Do you have any family to lean on?"

Riley faced her, eyes rimmed with pain. "I have no one left."

"I know what that's like." When she didn't have plans with Angela or Emily, Robin was alone.

"What about a father? Siblings?" Riley asked. "Or anyone else?"

Robin shook her head. "I was never lucky enough to meet the right one, and I'm an only child."

"Love has nothing to do with luck, and sometimes you must take a few wounds for it too. Love takes work."

Sometimes less work than she'd imagined. Robin snorted, remembering all the awful dates over the years. That counted as work. "You're right. It does."

"A woman like you must have friends waiting back home," he said with a hint of hopefulness.

"Yeah, I do." Robin dug in her purse and retrieved her phone. She hunched in disappointment as the glowing screen confirmed her fears.

"What is it?"

"No signal. I really am in the past."

"Just as I was really in the future. With you."

Robin swiped to bring up her photos. The battery was almost completely dead. "Here's me with Angela and Emily." She tilted the screen to his face, and pure wonder opened his eyes wide.

Robin chuckled. "I'm sorry for snarking at you about my phone at the festival. And it's not just a phone. It's camera too. I suppose you don't know what that is either. It, uh, captures a moment in time to save for later. I wonder what these two knuckleheads would say about this whole trip. Especially Emily. She would die for a chance to be on a pirate ship. That girl has a screw loose—" Robin cut herself off and glanced at Riley. "Sorry, I didn't mean..." she trailed off, wanting to change the subject.

Riley squinted.

"Sorry. I'm sorry. Sometimes it's easy to forget. Take a pic with me." She held the phone out and navigated to the camera mode. "Say cheese."

Robin pressed the button and looked at the captured image. Riley's face of shock and fear made her laugh. She showed him the image. "Now I'll always have a piece of you."

Riley smiled.

"Or at least until the battery dies."

"How can you preserve its life?"

She'd never heard someone think of it like that. "Without electricity and the proper charging cable, I can't."

"Sounds complicated."

"Lots of things are." Robin's gaze fell on the blood at his shoulder. "But this isn't. Your shoulder wound is still bleeding. Do you have a first aid kit so I can bandage it?"

"Bandages? Buckley knows where the doctor chest is."

Robin's features twisted. "The carpenter?"

"Who else? We haven't found a doctor willing to join the crew, and we haven't had luck finding one to press. We make do with what we have."

Robin checked his exposed skin for more injuries. He had a youthful glow on his firm skin, and his frame was wrapped in layers of muscle from the strenuous work of sailing a ship. He was younger than her by several years and simply beautiful.

Filthy.

But that was easily rectified.

She recalled again the glorious memory of Riley standing in her bathroom doorway, covered in a sheen of steam, holding nothing but her fluffy towel—an image she'd never forget—and then he'd dropped it. She wouldn't forget that either. Heat rushed up her cheeks. She needed to restore him to that glory, because it was her fault he was battered, bruised, and bleeding.

And he was single.

A KNOCK AT THE door had Robin moving across the room to answer it. Opening it a crack, she found Buckley had delivered a heavy chest. "I figured the captain was in need of medical attention, and that you'd prefer your privacy while attending him."

"Oh, thank you." Robin moved to take the chest from the carpenter, but he walked around her.

"Captain," he said, lowering the chest at Riley's feet. "You've made your case and proven your point. As much as the crew isn't happy about the situation, Robin should be safe now."

"Much obliged, Buckley," Riley said, dismissing him.

Buckley understood. He nodded at Robin and took his leave. Just before he crossed the threshold, he winked at her. Robin smiled in appreciation and closed the door.

"That was convenient," Robin said, kneeling at the chest and opening it.

"Buckley is a bit of a softy. How he tolerates such a crude living puzzles me, but he seems content."

Robin removed bandages that had seen better days, and a small bottle she sniffed and guessed was alcohol. It wasn't enough to sterilize the wounds, from what she remembered during her first aid training, but it was better than nothing.

She collected the torn, discarded tunic from the floor and bunched it up. Pressing it against the wound to staunch the flow, Robin said, "This shouldn't have happened."

"What?" Riley asked, gazing into her eyes.

"You getting hurt on my account."

"This?" Riley glanced at the fabric pressed on his wound. "This is nothing. A small cut is nothing against what would've happened had I lost."

Reading between the lines, Robin squinted and asked slowly, "You said you had full confidence."

Riley chuckled. "Did you see the size of him? His reach is longer than mine."

Robin's jaw dropped.

"Don't worry about it any longer. Being quick is usually better than being bigger."

"Usually," Robin mumbled, irritated that he'd gone into a fight so precarious and lied to her about it, so she wouldn't worry. And now she felt like an idiot. He protected her in more ways than one. For being a pirate, he was a gentleman. Robin's heart fluttered.

She pulled the fabric away, and the bleeding had slowed. She bandaged him up tightly. "How does that feel?"

"Better." He moved his arm around, testing its strength.

"Don't do that. You'll pull it open. You need as much rest as possible before this raid. How are you going to swing a sword now?" If Robin had it her way, he'd be on strict bed rest for weeks, but they didn't have that kind of time.

Riley collected the fresh tunic she'd pulled from the chest. She assisted him placing it over his head, allowing her fingertips to graze his skin.

"The same way I always do."

"And that is?"

"By knowing my life depended on it."

She hated when he spoke like that, like every minute could be his last. Due to weather, mutiny, a raid, or who knew what else, living on a ship during... "What year is it?"

"Seventeen-fifteen." He gestured for his belt, and Robin picked it up off the floor and wiped it down before handing it to him.

"I can't believe everything you told me was true." Robin fell back on the mattress next to him.

From what little of the past she'd experienced, it was the most dangerous time in history. The captain was injured. She was ill-prepared. And together they were heading into a guarded fort to steal their treasure. And still, she didn't know how many of the crew she could trust.

If they survived, she still had to go home.

Somehow.

21

Chapter 21

THE SHIP HUGGED THE river's bend, and Fort James closed in ahead, a sentry on the broad African river. As Riley had warned, cliffs on either riverbank meant no exit except on this ship, and the fort had a line of black cannons along the battlements. If the soldiers inside sniffed out Riley's intentions, the *Angelfish* wouldn't stand a chance against it.

And they would have nowhere to go.

Robin stood on the main deck at the rail, among the chosen few to accompany Riley into the fort. She was understandably jittery with nerves, waiting for Riley to return from his cabin. She didn't trust these men. Would they have their backs inside?

The raiding party had dressed in the best clothing they had, but only Riley and Robin wore jewelry. Riley also had feathers in his fancy hat, which no longer seemed silly, but quite fitting. Robin wore a gown from Riley's trunk, and it was foreign, uncomfortable, and way too hard to figure out how to put on. Her purse didn't match, but she refused to go anywhere without her pistol. On the bright side, the pretty layers made her feel like a princess at a ball. If she believed in fairytales.

She was starting to believe in unicorns.

With heat rushing her cheeks, Riley returned from his cabin, holding a small box, a jewelry box. "I have something for you."

"What is it?" Robin asked on a soft whisper of anticipation.

Riley opened the lid. A shiny ring with a stunning pattern carved in the gold. A wedding band. Robin's breath caught.

"I know what this looks like, but since we're pretending, we need to be as believable as possible. I've been saving this for years. I thought it was a shield, reminding me of what I lost to prevent that heartbreak from repeating. But... Instead, I think somewhere deep down, locked deep inside here I kept it out of hope." He touched his fist to his heart.

"Hope that somewhere, some*time*..." He paused, and his lips lifted in amusement. "A woman would unlock my heart, drag me from the abyss, and show me life was still worth living."

Robin smiled, wishing all that could be true for him.

"Robin, my dear, you're the one. You hold the key, and you showed me the light. You own my heart and soul from this day forth until my last breath. Will you be my wife?"

If only he didn't remind her of the pretend portion of their deal, it would've been much more swoony, but still Robin blinked away tears as if his words were real. She nodded and smiled, waiting until the clog of emotion in her throat cleared. It was almost too hard to accept on false pretenses, but this was what Riley said was needed to convince the commander. "Yes, I will."

With a warm smile of his own, Riley placed the ring on her finger. It was a little snug, but then she knew it would never be lost. She wanted a hug, a kiss, and a celebration of the joy between two people in love, but as the crew was watching and the proposal wasn't real, Riley returned to his duty.

"Raise the English ensign," Riley ordered in preparation for their arrival. "Let out the sheets and furl those sails."

Men staying behind sprung into action.

If things went wrong in there, the looming cannons weren't the only worry. Long before the commander would order the sinking of the *Angelfish*, she and Riley would be arrested for piracy, and all of them hung.

Riley shot her a smile as if calming her unspoken fears. His strong arm hugged her shoulder, keeping her on her feet. Facing a shooter on a public street with vehicles to take safety behind, a team at your back, and wearing armor was already stressful, but this was on a whole other level.

She was almost helpless. A few words were the difference between riches and gruesome death.

The men prepared a longboat for launch and a pair of oarsmen climbed inside, waiting to take them to shore.

Riley stepped forward and brought her knuckles to his lips. "You're next, my lovely wife."

Heat rushed up her cheeks, and her chest swelled. William Price chuckled behind them, ruining the moment by reminding her she was only pretending. She scowled at the towering, lanky man.

Riley held her hips while she crossed the open air to the swaying boat dangling by pulleys. Yet another boat—a smaller, weaker, less stable boat. Just great. She couldn't wait to plant her feet on solid ground again.

"Careful now. Wouldn't want to fall into the water. That dress is heavy." Riley said with a strange edge of worry in his voice.

"Of all things you need to concern yourself over, my ability to swim shouldn't even rank." Robin's movements shifted the weight of the boat, and it swayed drunkenly in the air. She lost her balance as she maneuvered and smacked her hip on the edge of her seat. "Ow."

Riley climbed in after and sat next to her, followed by the four accompanying them. He'd insisted they must be seen with servants from the household to be believable. Buckley the carpenter, Price the armorer, McKee the master gunner, and Cantu the behemoth joined them as escorts. Riley insisted he trusted these four with his life.

Vallo, who'd stood up for her, chose to stay on the ship with the quartermaster and all the men who'd showed her outright hatred. She'd made the right choice coming along.

"Lower us away," Buckley ordered after everyone was seated.

Her hands trembled as she gripped the rail of the boat. *Focus on land. Solid ground. Sand and dirt. Grass and stone.* The boat jerked and bounced as it neared the surface. The pair of rowers placed the oars in position and began stroking through the calm water. Riley held her hand.

"How certain are you this is going to work?" Buckley asked, hand resting on the hilt of his sword.

Riley cast her a side glance and squeezed her hand. "Sure enough to try."

Robin pressed her lips thin. "That's not very reassuring." And it was too late to go back. The crew would have their heads if they voluntarily returned to the ship without trying. As Riley said, cowards weren't tolerated.

"Where did you say you were from?" William Price asked. "There's something familiar about the way you speak."

Riley sent him a glare of death daggers, warning him to shut up. Price only smirked. The armorer seemed like the defiant type, so she wasn't surprised at his curiosity. Robin didn't know how to answer. Likely any mention of her visiting from the future would make them all laugh at her. They didn't need a distraction right now. Understanding Riley's warning look, she said, "I'm not from around here."

"Indeed," Price said. "I think you're being obtuse on purpose. Not so long ago, I met a woman—"

"Enough," Riley interrupted. "We are walking into enemy territory in disguise. We need to focus."

"Some of us are perfectly capable of holding a conversation while battle looms ahead," Price said.

"Battle?" Robin asked.

"He speaks figuratively," Riley said, brow darkening. "And dangerously."

"I beg your pardon," Price said casually. "You're too tightly wound, captain. You remind me of my brother Henry, and it's not a good look on anyone. Only a few weeks ago you were as laid back about this plan as I am now. Something's changed."

Riley stiffened at her side.

"Leave the captain alone," Cantu said.

McKee rolled his eyes. "Price is right." Turning to the captain, he added, "Relax, captain. It's the only way this half-cocked plan is going to work. A wealthy merchant is dauntless and confident. Right now, you're shaking like a leaf."

Robin focused on the captain's hand. He was not shaking. These men were teasing him, but why?

"You're both right," Buckley said and glanced at McKee. "Riley, you need to loosen your nerves and lighten up, but we all need to take this situation seriously. There's a lot of soldiers in there and only a few of us. This is a battle of words, and the odds are not in our favor."

Robin frowned. "What do you mean?"

Riley squeezed her hand quickly but glared at the others in the boat. "The plan is perfect, but it takes men acting responsibly to pull it off."

"It takes a man acting married." Buckley winked.

Heat rushed up Robin's cheeks, and Riley cleared his throat.

The other men chuckled at their discomfort. Jerks.

"It's the curse," one of the rowers said. The laughter stopped, and the men focused on the rower. He added, "Our crew is cursed. Ever since Lemoine became captain of the *Sea Lion*, we've been cursed. You should've warned the new recruits what they're in for."

"What curse?" Robin asked, a disbeliever in the occult until she'd fallen through time. The men had whispered about a curse, but no one explained what it meant.

"It's making our captains go soft," the other rower said grimly.

Taking offense, Riley shot him a nasty glare.

McKee laughed. "There's nothing wrong with choosing a warm woman in your bed over a ship full of unwashed bilge rats."

"Because there's a time you'd choose a cold woman?" Cantu asked.

"If I must have a woman at all, a cold, aloof woman between dawn and dusk is preferable," Price said, glib. "But as McKee said, I'd prefer a warm woman in my bed, too, as long as she understood to leave in the morning."

Robin scowled at Price's disregard for women. Clearly he'd had a few bad experiences. The men laughed, and she glared at Riley, who covered his amusement. In reality, their teasing was mild compared to what she'd heard on a daily basis at the police station.

The boat slid to a stop on shore and immediately the nerves returned, but her feet couldn't wait to reach the sand.

"I hate to ask this, captain, but is there a signal or point in time you want us to turn back for the *Angelfish*?" one of the rowers asked slowly.

"If you hear yelling or gunshots, return to the ship. Notify Randall. It is his decision to proceed or abandon the raid," Riley said smoothly, as if that had always been his plan.

"Wait. If we need help, they're going to leave?" Robin asked. The true stakes of this endeavor hadn't been revealed to her.

Riley gripped her hands. "If the captain is lost, the quartermaster is in charge until a new one is chosen. I cannot fault the men for leaving us, but if they do, they're stupid. Buckley is a fine carpenter and the best the crew has. Cantu has great power and loyalty. McKee leads the gun crew, and Price..." the captain trailed off. While Riley searched the thin man's weathered face with a relaxed posture, the other men's chests puffed with pride. "Price is a special guy who's great at keeping things sharp."

"You are correct on all points, captain," Price said. "But you're forgetting one thing."

"What's that?" McKee asked.

"Randall is new to the crew. As much as we all elected him our leader, how much can we trust him? Landry is still there. And I heard all the stories about Vallo. I don't know why he's been so agreeable lately," Price said.

"I don't trust them either," Riley said. "Which is why they aren't here. I don't need either one of them messing up our plans. Besides, the dozens of men on board can keep them in line."

"Let's hope you're right," McKee said.

The men climbed out of the boat, and Riley assisted her careful steps. Feet firmly planting on solid land, Robin didn't feel as good as she thought she would. The fort neared like an unpredictable, dangerous hive.

Taking a few deep breaths to unwind her twisted stomach, she smoothed the layers of her dress and hooked her arm under Riley's. Together they marched with their servants behind them to poke the nest.

Chapter 22

BEFORE THE WOMAN ON his arm appeared in his life, Riley was sure, steady, and confident in the upcoming steps necessary to meet the ends he'd planned—riches for the crew, but the return to Gwyneth, her brother, and Riley's father for him.

Now leading Robin toward an unknown fate, Riley returned her worried smile to comfort her. For the first time, he no longer pined for the relationship he now understood he wore blinders for. The real thing was right before him, and that was the problem. The risk to Robin's life, coupled with the crew's teasing had him worried more than her. Riley had chosen his men well, but if the uncharacteristic teasing slipped during the meeting, their entire operation would be compromised.

Servants didn't jest with their masters.

And then Riley would never get to tell Robin what he wanted to say during his pretend proposal.

The guards at the gate were heavily armed and well-nourished. With one last look over his shoulder at the *Angelfish* anchored in the middle of the river, Riley approached. Using the heavy English accent from his childhood, he said, "Captain Riley, merchant. Here for an appointment with Commander Mitchell, if you please."

The guards exchanged glances, and the first one nodded. He turned and shouted to open the gate. The creaking heavy doors spread wide like the hungry mouth of the kraken, ready to devour its next morsel.

Just inside the monstrous door, a man in fine clothing held his hands folded in front of him, waiting for their entry. "Right this way." He turned to lead them into the belly of the fort.

Riley held Robin tightly to his side, and his men followed on their heels. The courtyard was larger than it looked from the outside, and as hoped, they'd arrived in time for lunch. The soldiers were not on the perimeter battlement. According to his information, close to a hundred soldiers were stationed here.

The crew was ushered into a spacious room with a long table and plenty of light. Two soldiers stood guard at the door. The commander, wearing an extraordinary hat and many decorations of service, waited with his hands clasped together.

The raiding party, finally taking on the role of servants, spread out, as if ready to spring to Riley's every need. They kept their eyes on the floor and their mouths closed.

The commander offered his hand to shake, and Riley took it.

"I received your letter. This must be your curious wife. She's lovely."

Heat rushed up Riley's cheeks. If only she would be... "You're too kind, sir."

"Well, I'll admit I was skeptical at first, but you've convinced me to hear you out. Please have a seat. As for your servants of highest regard, I imagine they haven't eaten properly in weeks. If it pleases you, Captain, I'll invite them to the table with us."

Riley suppressed his surprise. The man was beyond reasonable, or he had very high expectations and wanted to impress Riley. Either way, he had to be careful.

"It does," Riley said. "Your extraordinary kindness is noted."

The commander nodded and everyone took a place at the table. Riley never released Robin's hand, and he never intended to until they were out of the building.

At once, a cart was pushed into the room. As Riley's crew watched the goings on, the commander said, "Sweetmeat, seasoned potatoes, and tea are on the menu. I hope it shall suffice."

The crew hid their smiles of approval. Soon the commander wouldn't be as generous.

"It shall," Riley said, pretending to not be impressed by the spread.

Real servants set out food around the table, a setting for each person.

The commander tucked a napkin over his cravat and lifted his fine silverware. "Your request said you wish to enslave natives. Is that correct?"

Riley shifted his fingers to spin the ring around Robin's finger. Hopefully she understood this conversation wasn't real. "How many can you have available for me by this time next week?"

The commander chuckled merrily. "In a hurry, I see."

Buckley, McKee, and Price attacked their plates with the hunger of sailors caught for weeks becalmed at sea. Cantu was more reserved, carefully observing before tasting.

Robin didn't touch hers. Riley leaned down to her ear and whispered, "Go ahead. It'll be the best meal you've had for a while."

"Pardon?" the commander asked.

Riley smiled politely, "I was telling the missus there's no need to be shy."

Commander Mitchell spoke with his mouth full, "We are hearty men. Dig in, my lady. Enjoy the fruits of everyone else's labors." He swallowed and laughed.

Cantu lifted a forkful of meat to his lips.

Robin cringed at the food. As he'd struggled to swallow the 'burger' from the future, she stared at the dish before her. There was nothing more he could say to encourage her without giving himself away.

Reluctantly, Riley released her hand and finally tasted the offering himself. It was most excellent. The finest in sweetmeat, seasoned to perfection, and buttered bread with sweetened tea. Not able to help himself, Riley inhaled his food as his crew did.

"Let me hear this proposal of yours." The commander belched into his napkin.

And everyone believed pirates had no manners.

Pausing from his most hearty meal, Riley said, "My hold is vast enough to carry thirty slaves. I'm seeking strong men and a few boys to work my plantation. If we can reach an accord, I shall return in three months' time for another thirty. I'm paying top dollar for the best you can find."

"A sugar merchant?"

"That is correct."

"Why did you bring your wife to a man's business deal?" the commander asked.

Robin's face darkened, but she refrained from objecting, and Riley didn't like that note of suspicion. Off the top of his head, he expanded on the fib given in his letter. "She wanted to see more of the world, and she has a fondness for the Crown's forts. Isn't that right, my lady? And I can never turn down my lady's wishes." He gazed into her eyes and smiled warmly. For that he didn't have to act. Robin smiled back, but she was nervous. He'd expected that.

William Price's comment had been correct. Before Robin had become part of this plan, Riley had been confident and at ease about it. Now he was nervous, too.

Buckley smiled with a mouthful like an old coot. Price snorted, and when the commander darted him a look, Price said, "My apologies, commander. My digestive tract is articulating its appreciation for such a fine spread."

The commander nodded, accepting the apology.

Cantu was impassive. He still ate, but slowly and carefully. McKee finished his plate on time. Riley's trusty master gunner stood at once. "If you'll excuse my own digestive tract, I must attend the toilet. Please direct me accordingly and pardon my untimely interruption. It was not my intention."

The commander pointed to the door. "Between my men there and to the left. Ignore the rowdy soldiers in the Great Hall. We don't have visitors frequently enough to polish their manners."

McKee bowed properly and left.

Excellent.

Price and Cantu finished their plates much quicker now. Robin ate what she could stomach, and Riley didn't mind her pickiness. He'd hardly kept down the 'burger'. What an odd food that was.

"How were the winds on your journey?" the commander asked.

"Full and expedient." Now it was Riley's turn to ask questions. "A marvelous fort you have here. How many men do you keep in these high walls?"

"Forty, give or take. A good third of them are in training. Whipping these boys into any form of moldable man is quite the task."

That was also excellent. "My lady here is fascinated. She wants to know how you can defend the fort with so few hands."

"The parapets are high and the walls thick," Commander Mitchell answered Riley without looking at Robin. "Getting inside the reinforced iron door is nigh impossible. So long as the enemy stays out there, we're safe in here, as I'm sure your lady is happy to hear."

Robin smiled politely and nodded, accepting the commander's slight as she set her napkin near her plate. Riley was sure she raged beneath her calm exterior, but he was impressed with her performance. The commander was about to receive a few knocks to his bloated ego.

Riley finished his meal, and McKee returned from the toilet and nodded.

Time to make the move.

With a careful eye on the pair of soldiers, Riley pulled his pistol from his bandolier and aimed at their host. The soldiers motioned for their own weapons. "Commander, please order your men to stand down."

Next to him Robin gasped. Riley hadn't given her the details of the plan, because he didn't want her to stop him, and he needed her reaction to be authentic. If they lost their attempt to take the fort, she could be spared. A long shot, but the chance was worth the deception.

The crew drew their weapons, and the commander visibly shook with shock and anger. After a long glare of indecision, which would set their fate's course, the commander said, "Do as our guest orders."

Riley smiled, but no one relaxed. "I knew you were a smart man. Now, the location of the hold, if you will."

The commander's mouth gaped open. "When the rest of my soldiers discover what you've done, they'll hang you."

"They're busy," McKee said. "You're on your own."

"But..." the commander trailed off, confused.

"The Great Hall has a great lock," McKee said with a self-satisfied grin.

Riley said, "Commander, tell us the whereabouts of the hold and allow us to leave in peace and no one shall be hurt."

"You're...you're..." He looked from one face to the next genuinely hurt. As he took in their appearance more closely and studied their weapons, Commander Mitchell's features twisted. "Pirates?"

"The hold, commander." Riley stood and waved his pistol to urge his tongue. The other pirates rose. "I recommend not giving your life for King George's pocket change."

The commander lifted his hands in surrender and sweat beaded on his forehead. "I'll lead you."

Chapter 23

THE CAPTAIN KEPT STRIDE with the commander, keeping the gun visible as if the man needed a reminder to behave. Robin followed Riley closely, hand in her purse gripping her Glock. The commander's steps were stilted as if he warred with the decision to comply with the pirates' demands.

For a moment, she wished the jerk would make a wrong move, but his rudeness abruptly vanished once a gun was trained on his head. Under duress, people sometimes reacted in unexpected ways, and she was glad the commander turned to jelly rather than take the offensive.

Robin realized she'd been jelly, freezing during her home invasion, leading to her mom's death, freezing during a bank shootout, causing her colleague's death, and Robin had choked again when Riley fought to the death with his challenger, Kerr.

Robin was not jelly anymore.

Men rattled the Great Hall's doors, shouting in confusion and worry.

The commander stared at the door and slowed his steps as they approached.

"It's in your best interest to keep moving, Commander Mitchell," Riley said with a dark tone. He pressed the barrel of his pistol in the commander's side.

The commander wiped sweat from his brow and nodded, resuming his steps. The crew followed, working as a practiced unit—watching each other's backs, keeping an eye out for soldiers above, and aiming at every open passage. Their coordination was impressive. They'd make a great tactical unit if they were on the other side of the law.

The commander led them down a spiral stairwell into the dank and dim underbelly of the fort. At the bottom, the commander stopped. The mossy scent had Robin concerned over ventilation and air quality down here. Hopefully they weren't staying long. Ahead of the commander stood a heavy door with a barred window in the center. Beyond the door was a corridor of iron gates, and from what she could see, shelves full of wood crates. If she ever pictured a castle's dungeon, this was it.

"Through this door is the hold. The keys are hanging there." Mitchell pointed to a rusty ring mounted into the wall.

Riley smiled. "You made the right choice here. Men!"

Buckley collected the keys and unlocked the door, while Cantu and McKee gripped the commander firmly under the arms.

Price sidled up next to Robin. "You're doing fine. Keep it together a little longer."

Robin frowned at Price. "I don't need a pep talk."

"Suit yourself. I only wanted to stop you from waving that strange weapon of yours. The sound would be unfortunate."

Robin frowned and pulled her arm out of her purse. It wasn't like she was reckless with the thing. She had only tried to help.

"You can't do this! I did everything you asked. Let me go, I beg of you!" The commander whined and panted with fear, but he didn't put up much of a struggle.

Ignoring the pleas, the crew passed through the hold's main door, and ushered the commander to the first cell. Buckley unlocked the gate.

"No, please, no. Anything. I'll do anything you ask, but not this. Please don't do this!"

Cantu and McKee shoved the commander in. He promptly lost his footing and landed on his knees. Buckley locked him in place, and the commander rushed back to the bars and held them like he was going to continue begging. He didn't. Only the withdrawn look of fear twisted his features.

Robin's stomach swirled. Pirates in action, hurting people for their own gain. She didn't like it, but she didn't stop them either. Her only focus was making sure Riley got out of this fort alive.

The carpenter rattled the keys with a grin. "Let's see this immeasurable wealth waiting for us."

Price held up a metal pin with disappointment on his face. A pin Robin recognized, and confusion knitted her brows.

"And here I brought this bobby pin to pick the lock, marvelous thing, but I didn't need it. Such a shame." He dropped it into his pocket and closed in around the gate with the others.

Buckley unlocked the next gate, and it swung open on squeaky hinges. The men rushed to the crates, ripping them open with bare hands. Price found a metal bar nearby, and he pried the trickier lids. Metal coins rattled, and Price giggled with pure joy.

Genuine happiness.

A sound so foreign to Robin.

Burlap flew in the air and more of the men laughed.

It was contagious. Robin's lips spread wide, happy for them.

"Take what you can carry but don't injure yourself. We'll need several trips. Congratulations, men," Riley said.

The crew nodded to Riley with beaming grins as they walked out with arms full. Robin picked up a sack and flung it over her shoulder.

Riley's smile slid away. "What are you doing?"

"I'm helping. The sooner we get out of here, the better."

Riley considered for a long moment. "If we're caught, plead with them. Explain that I forced you. Can you do that for me?"

He was asking her to sacrifice him to save herself. After all she'd been through, not a chance. But since the stakes were precarious right now, Robin said, "Deal."

Satisfied, Riley picked up a crate, and they ascended the stairs together. Through the corridors, across the courtyard, and beyond the Great Hall with angry shouts and rhythmic pounding on the doors, Riley and Robin reached the shore. Arms full, Robin set down the sack on the sand. She shielded her eyes against the fading sun. Riley set down the crate.

The longboat was gone, but the *Angelfish* was still at anchor.

"They are coming back, right?" Robin asked.

"The load they carried was only a tease. The soldiers are locked down, and the doors to the vault are wide open. They'd never sail away from such an easy target."

Robin was grateful for a moment's privacy. "I've been meaning to ask you something."

"Go ahead." Riley turned to gaze into her eyes, ignoring the ship entirely.

"How did you get to the future?"

Riley's face displayed his confusion as he searched his memories. "All I remember is picking up a shiny necklace out of the sand in Nassau, confronting a traitor, and...that's it."

Riley went both ways. The secret had to be with him somewhere. "What about how you returned here?"

"Let's see. I was dressing in your home. I put on my cocked hat." Riley paused, considering. "No, I took off my hat and put on the..." he trailed off.

"The necklace," she finished for him, excitement growing in her voice as she worked through her own path. "I bought one from a vendor, and when I was walking in the grass, I put it on. That's how I ended up here. How is it possible two magic necklaces are floating around? Did that vendor know what she was selling? I remember she said to me, 'Amethyst has been known to grant your truest desire while protecting you from bad humors, so be careful how you use it.' I dismissed it as occult superstition, but she was telling the truth."

"What was your truest desire?" Riley asked with heat behind his eyes.

Robin dug through her thoughts at the time and snorted a laugh. "A unicorn. I wanted a unicorn, which I didn't believe existed."

She believed now.

Riley tilted his head, completely lost, while he dug through the layers of his fine clothing and showed his pendant on a chain. "I'm not sure I follow."

Robin copied, showing her matching pendant to his, and laughed. "I'm not crazy. They're identical; they're magic. And since you went both ways..." Robin trailed off as the excitement drifted away.

"You can go home," Riley finished for her.

She glanced at the gold ring on her finger. It was a little too snug, but it felt right like it belonged. "I can't."

Riley faced her, eyes flashing between excitement and worry. "The raid is a success, if not yet complete. The crew is satisfied, so there's no reason for you to risk your life in my world any longer. I must insist you return home to your own life, to what you know."

Riley's plea to leave him stung, and she fought back tears. His promise might've been fulfilled to the crew, but she wasn't finished yet. Robin smiled softly. "There's a reason I can't."

Riley peered into her eyes, waiting patiently.

Robin glanced away to compose herself. Whether he wanted her in his life for real, that didn't change her resolve. "I made you a promise, and I won't break it. There's a traitor on that ship, and I'm not leaving until I know you're safe. There's nothing you can say to change my mind."

Riley sighed and closed his eyes in defeat. "Promise me this. Promise me when I'm safe, you'll go home."

Swallowing a lump of emotion, Robin said, "I promise."

A crushing weight settled in her chest. Would that be the one promise she made with the intention of breaking? Only if the stubborn man wanted her as much as she wanted him!

At least she bought herself more time to convince him they could make this work.

Chapter 24

THE LONGBOAT HAD RETURNED several times over, and with wide open gates, extra pirates joined to speed the collection of the treasure. Robin made trips in and out of the hold, piling the sand high with crates and burlap sacks for the men to load up, not willing to leave Riley's side.

All this weight and all those crates...trip after trip. There had to be hundreds if not a thousand pounds of silver. Robin had never seen so much, and during their hunt for the last of the cache, they'd found a stash of wine. The pirates confiscated all of it, and several bottles were guzzled at once in a sea of laughter while the rest were squirreled away on the longboats for later. Before departing the fort for good, the crew fired off the guns on the perimeter battlements in celebration.

At least, in their merry state of drunkenness, they didn't hit the ship. Sometimes luck came in weird ways.

At the end of the day, the *Angelfish* drifted back down river, loaded with a lifetime's worth of treasure, and most of the men on board were completely smashed, but the rigging crew abstained until their shift was over. Someone still had to sail the ship out of the precarious river. As much as she hated boats, she much preferred the *Angelfish* to taking her chances with a fort full of angry soldiers, who still rattled the Great Hall doors as they left.

Robin gripped the edge of the table in the mess hall below deck to steady herself. Unlike the crew, she still wasn't used to the movement. Several men she hadn't met shared the table, but Riley sat next to her, and Cantu and McKee were across from her.

"What a mighty fine plunder we found, captain! A most successful raid. I didn't think it possible," McKee said and chugged down his mug of wine.

"I'll admit, the drink on this ship has improved," Cantu said, smiling.

That Robin could agree with. She sipped from her mug, stomach sloshing from the movement, and although she wished for water, the wine was better than ale, punch, or rum.

"Are you well?" Riley asked her. "You've been quiet."

"I hate boats, mix my stomach with wine, and I'm a little unsettled. No more wine for me."

"Why on earth do you hate boats?" McKee asked, brows raised in astonishment.

"I was on one a few years ago. Everyone was drinking." She pointedly looked at those around her.

"Sounds like a good time," Cantu said. He and McKee banged mugs and drank.

"They drank too much," Robin added, and the others listened. "A small fight rocked the boat, and everyone tried to break them up. One thing led to another, and most of us went overboard."

"That's no good," McKee said.

"It was dark. I was a good swimmer, and a few of my friends, too, but a few of us never made it back to the surface. Alcohol and water never mix well."

Riley rested his hand on her lap. "I had no idea."

"It didn't seem like a relevant point to bring up." She didn't need to give Riley another reason to insist she went home, so she'd kept it to herself.

"It's a good thing this ship is strong and study. No one's going in the water unless they want to," McKee said. "Or we make them."

She hoped that was true.

"Honestly, captain, I didn't think you were going to pull it off," Bauer said from the end of the table. Robin hadn't heard him speak before, but his fluid voice matched that of his beautiful singing voice.

Still didn't compare to Riley's. His voice in the shower was captivating.

"Me neither. But I'm damned glad you did!" Gunner, the scrawny teenager said and laughed.

Riley smiled and nodded. Others laughed.

"To endless wealth," Watts said, raising his mug. Cantu, McKee, Karl, and Price joined him. "And endless women and booze."

Robin frowned.

The men clinked mugs and drank, spilling wine down their faces. Nothing could ruin the crew's mood, and for once, Robin felt perfectly safe around them, Glock or not. She smiled and clasped her hands around the mug.

Buckley curled into a seat at the table on Robin's other side. "I'll drink to that every day. Maybe you're not the curse we thought. Perhaps this time, you're a good luck charm."

Riley stared at Buckley with that same death gaze. Robin's curiosity drew her in. "What do you mean by 'this time'?"

"You're not the first woman on board," Buckley said. "Not even the second."

That was what Giles meant when he'd said, 'A *woman popping out of the hold*.' If others had been here before her, their surprise, fury, and insult at her appearance was unfounded...and infuriating. "And yet you treated me like some thief stealing passage."

"Men don't change easily," Cantu said. "Especially when you have new crew members." He darted a look at Vallo, Green, and Landry who shared a different table with the quartermaster.

"He's right," Riley said. "These men before you are familiar with the phenomenon. Those aren't. And a divide of the crew is difficult to manage. It always leads to conflicts and unwanted skirmishes."

Remembering her own random appearance on the ship, perhaps these men knew more about this mystical occurrence than she did. Maybe she'd find out what happened to those women. "What do you know about the curse?"

"It's witchcraft," McKee said. "As long as it keeps us in women, I'm bound to get one eventually, so I have no qualms."

Giles had told her the same sentiment. Men laughed.

"Every time a new captain has been voted in, a woman appears on board. The captain leaves us for her. Once was unfortunate. Twice a coincidence." Cantu sipped from his mug and stared her down. His eyes flicked to Riley for a second. "I no longer believe in coincidence."

Riley said nothing.

"Why are you looking at me like that?" Robin sipped from her mug to hide her face.

"You know why."

They assumed she was going to steal Riley from them and do what? She didn't live here. Riley's home was this ship, and there was no way she'd consider this pile of boards to be home. How crazy of an idea was that? How preposterous? How...? Robin was done drinking. More wine would only loosen her up more. The last thing she needed was to lose control.

"Well, I think I've had enough drink for the night. Robin, care to join me?" Riley held out his palm.

Several of the crew smiled knowingly. A couple cackled.

Robin took his hand, and he led her up to and across the main deck. Guess there'd be no dancing tonight. The idea bummed her out.

"Tonight," Riley said, stopping at his cabin door, "you're staying with me the whole night."

Robin relished the idea, but... "But what about the crew?"

"They're fed, drunk, and buried in so much silver they can't think straight. We'll be left alone."

"If you think so." The last thing she wanted was to be caught in bed. Rules were rules, regardless of riches. At least, that was the crew's whole problem with her. "You're a rich man now, captain. So what do you plan to do with all your plunder?"

Riley cast her a knowing grin and gestured for her to follow him inside. Robin did. Closed into together, he stalked up to her with hunger and desperation in his eyes. He brought his face close to hers, and his hands reached for her throat, thumbs skimming her jaw. "The only plunder I want is right in front of me." He paused, and demanded quietly, "Kiss me."

He didn't have to ask twice.

Robin's lips found his, and she pressed her body against the firm muscles beneath his layers of clothing. One by one, she stripped off the pieces covering his fine torso and released them. Riley reached around her and worked the buttons of her ill-fitting dress, while she ran her bare palms up the curves of his chest, from the rigid abs flexing with his movements to his pectorals, flickering from the effort. She kissed his throat in a teasing line, and Riley paused for a moment to groan.

Robin smiled from her prowess affecting him so.

The dress tore free and fell to the floor.

She wore her modern underwear, and Riley took a long look at her. The corners of his lips lifted. "Simply beautiful."

With a soft laugh, she said, "Shut up and get over here."

Riley scooped her up in his arms and settled her on the mattress. Looming over her and gazing at her with the hunger of a starved man, Riley worked at the ties fastening his breeches. Robin assisted. Once the knot worked free, she pushed the material down. Riley leaned upright on his knees and shrugged out of his drawers.

She drank in his beautiful, towel-free body, and it was simply divine.

Robin lifted her hips and slipped off her underwear. "Come here before I get cold."

A sly smile touched his lips. "Unlike Price, I only want a warm woman in my life, even if that means I have to work you all night to keep you hot."

Robin grabbed his neck and pulled him down. "Time's a-wastin'," she sang deviously.

Riley growled and positioned himself. His mouth found her body, and he paid attention to every heightened nerve on her skin, making her sing for him.

Captain Riley didn't quit until he sated the delicious throbbing pooling between her legs, and even though Robin begged him to deliver the thrusts faster, to climb that pleasure mountain quicker, Riley kept her quiet by capturing her lips as the explosive orgasm contracted every muscle in her body.

Sex was forbidden on this ship, but Robin couldn't have waited any longer. She loved him, and she could never let him go.

A POUNDING ON THE cabin door pulled Robin upright. The sheet fell away, exposing her breasts. Riley sat up, bleary-eyed, but he perked up when he caught an eyeful.

"You're the most beautiful and appreciated morning view I've ever had."

Robin smiled.

The pounding repeated.

"Something's going on out there," Robin said. "And they don't sound happy."

Riley climbed out of bed and dressed.

Unable to waste time on the excessive buttons, Robin found her previous dress from Riley's trunk and slipped it over her head. They dressed quickly together, chuckling softly like busted teens.

"What do you suppose it is?" she asked, balling up the fancy dress and dropping it into the chest. Hoping Riley had been right about their nighttime escapades being overlooked.

"Not sure." Riley tied his breeches while glancing out the cabin's windows and squinted in the rising dawn. "By now we should be leaving the mouth of the river, so from here out we should have smooth sailing back to Nassau for a couple weeks. Doesn't look like the weather is a concern." Riley fastened his weapons belt and slipped into his boots.

After a quick glance over his shoulder to make sure Robin was covered, he nodded, and stepped out.

Robin only needed an extra minute before she followed. On the main deck, the men gathered near his door. This time, Landry led the charge.

"A duel wasn't enough to scare the captain straight," Landry said, addressing the crew while snarling at the captain. "Silver and wine aren't enough to bribe me. Clearly the captain's got his head in the wrong place, and we need to do something about it."

Not again. Didn't Riley's success over Kerr and the raid on the fort mean anything to these monsters?

"Ah, there she is," Landry said, spotting her in the crowd. "The object of Riley's distraction. Last chance, captain. Either she accompanies me to my hammock this moment, or I officially call a duel. You and me or her and me. The choice is yours."

Robin wanted to know how Landry could confidently wield a sword with so many fingers missing, but if the man was brave enough to publicly challenge Riley, he had a reason to expect he'd win. As worried as Robin was about the treasure having no impact on the crew's view of her, she was morbidly curious.

"I don't think so," Vallo said, pushing his way through the gathered crowd.

Landry stared at the short man with hatred. "What did you say to me?"

"You're not challenging the captain. He's done a great job with this account. Regardless of the status of his...breeches...he's a remarkable captain."

Riley stared at him, completely baffled. Although Robin had experienced Vallo's support, this was a higher level than she'd expected considering Riley didn't trust the man.

"Oh, and what are you going to do about it?" Landry sneered.

With a quick movement no one saw coming, Vallo unsheathed his sword and buried it deep into Landry's scrawny neck. Robin flinched in surprise, as did half the crew. Riley's eyes widened.

A calm smile crossed Vallo's lips, and he pulled his sword free. Landry fell to the deck with a wet thump.

"Now, can we continue the celebrations?" Vallo asked.

The crew whispered to each other, deciding what to do next.

Green pushed his way through and scowled at his downed friend, displaying the revolting teeth in his mouth. "I say we hold an election this instant."

Robin's spirits sunk. Riley had told her the only thing standing between the crew and her was his sword, but if he lost the captaincy, the new captain's rules were fair game.

She trusted Riley, but she didn't believe he could dispatch every man who insisted on taking her to bed.

"Now—" Riley started.

"A new quartermaster," Bauer, the night watch crooner interrupted and winked at Riley. "Some of us feel Vallo fits the position better. He knows what's best for the crew, and he's willing to act on it. So I say cheers! All those in favor?"

More whispers followed before the cumulative "Ayes" filled the air.

Vallo smiled and bowed. "Thank you all kindly."

Randall pushed his way through, a nasty scowl filling his features. "What did I hear?"

Vallo said with a smug smile, "You're out. I'm the quartermaster now."

Randall opened his mouth to object when a man high above in the rigging shouted, "Sails!"

Heads turned up, looking for the direction. At once the celebrations of the successful raid and the change in vote ended. Soberness took over as if they hadn't spent the night enjoying the bottom of many, many wine bottles.

Something was wrong.

Chapter 25

HEAD REELING WITH CONFUSION and alarm from the abrupt change of quartermaster to a known traitor, Riley relished the day watchman's interruption. Just outside the mouth of the river, with bluffs all along the coast, a ship was closing in from somewhere. Riley concentrated, squinting into the night, and there... She was there. His eyes widened as he scrambled for the spyglass. He pressed it to his eye and sucked in a breath. The faintest glow of the coming dawn outlined her.

Peibo del ler San Francisco.

But how?

Riley gave his orders for a full sail with urgency. Their two advantages were draft and speed. They had to outrun her. They had no other choice.

"What is it? Who are they, uh, she?" Robin asked, approaching the rail at Riley's side.

Riley turned to her. The moonlight bathed her worried face. "An old enemy. That ship has no reason to head this way. Someone must've disclosed our course ahead of time."

He had only one guess who it was, but after Vallo's uncharacteristic friendliness to the crew, Riley couldn't accuse him otherwise. If the crew survived this encounter,

Riley would see the traitor's punishment meted out with his own hands.

"Are they pirates too?" Robin asked, confused.

If only.

"*Peibo del ler San Francisco*, a Spanish warship captained by a man who has a history with our crew and a thorn in his side, a one *Capitán* Delgado. He's ruthless, he's angry, and he's been embarrassed. We're tacking along the coast. With the shallow draft of the schooner, it's our best chance to stay out of range."

But they were heavily weighed down with treasure from the fort.

"And if they enter the range needed?" Robin asked, voice shaking.

Riley didn't want to lie to her. "God help us."

Robin hugged Riley's middle and watched with him as the enemy sails became clearer to see. The *Peibo del ler San Francisco* followed their course precisely. The *Angelfish* had been spotted.

Riley hated that Robin stood here on this deck with battle looming once again, but this time their odds of survival were lower than slim.

A dull ache pressed against his chest, making breathing difficult. He had to issue the order at the cost of his own happiness. Riley choked back emotion until he could speak. He gathered her hands in his. "Robin, listen to me closely. Our schooner is severely outgunned. That's a warship. If we are forced to fight, we will lose." He pushed her to arm's reach and stared into her eyes. "Do you understand me?"

"I get it, but there must be some way out of this." She craned her neck, searching for an answer, but one side was open ocean with a warship and the other side was nothing but sheer bluffs. He saw no other answer.

Riley blinked rapidly. He'd risked her life too many times already. This wasn't a risk; this was certain death. "I want you to leave. Understand me? I need to know you're safe. Take off the necklace, and put it back on."

"I...I can't leave you like this. I promised, and I won't go back on it now." Robin pulled out of his grip.

Heart breaking, he begged, "If you stay, you'll die, and I can't live with myself knowing I did this to you. Please return to the safety of your home. I want you to live. That's enough for me."

"My decision to stay is not your fault. And why are you so doom-and-gloom? Your own crew said you have more experience on a pirate ship than any man here. Fight back, escape, do whatever it is you always do to win." Tears leaked down her cheeks.

A cannon fired, the boom echoing against the cliff. Robin covered her ears, and the splintering bang and screams hollowed Riley. He couldn't stand this. He wouldn't allow this. He reached for her throat and lifted the necklace over her head. Robin dove for his hand in a panic.

"Gun crews at the ready!" Captain ordered, and McKee carried the words to his men, who scrambled.

Another boom followed the first, and the chain shot severed a mast. Splinters flew. Wood cracked and creaked. The mainmast, tangled in lines, groaned as it toppled.

Their ship was a dead stick in the water.

"Open fire!" Riley ordered.

McKee took command of his gun crew, and guns exploded in retaliation, the booms deafening. While Riley was distracted with the orders, Robin stole the necklace from his hand.

Riley returned to face her. "We lost the main, and the hull is next. You need to go or we all drown."

Robin sniffled with the necklace in her fist. "I said I'm not leaving. If you want to use yours to escape, I'll go with you. Until then, I'm staying here by your side." Staring him in the eye, she threw the necklace overboard.

Riley fastened his palms against her cheeks as booms of guns fired both ways. Wood crunched and splinters flew. Injured men screamed. "Stupid. That was stupid, Robin. Can't you see? We won't survive this."

Her hands wrapped over his, and she sobbed. "I'm not leaving you."

The ship listed. Men cried out. Candles snuffed out from the splashing water.

The ship was going down. Hopefully so close to shore, the water wasn't too deep.

Riley couldn't swim.

SHE WAS STUPID, BUT she was stupidly and stubbornly going to save Riley. The ship tilted severely. Robin lost her balance and tumbled. Riley gripped a rail and continued shouting his orders over the deafening noise. Keeping her Glock around her body like a lifeline, Robin caught onto the opposite rail and gripped it with all her strength. A cannon ball blew a hole in the rail near her, but she didn't get hit with any splinters. She still yelped in surprise.

The ship's tilt meant their port cannons pointed toward the water, useless to fire. The ones on the other side of the deck rolled uncontrollably backward, aiming in the wrong direction. They were useless, too. Water climbed the deck. Men rushed up from below with weapons tucked into their sashes and belts.

"There's nothing more we can do, captain," Cantu said. "She's going down. The *Angelfish* is lost."

Robin climbed away from the rising waters toward Riley, but the slickness of the ocean spray and lack of handholds left her sliding. Robin climbed on all fours, knees catching on her dress. Around her, men fell into the water. Some splashed, shouting for help. Others sank quietly.

Robin reached Riley's side. "Stay on the ship as long as possible."

"Aye," Riley said. His tone carried defeat.

Smoke from the gunpowder obscured the growing dawn's light, and slowly the cannon fire stopped. As the water filled the hull, the ship's angle straightened out and water rushed over their feet.

"It's going to suck us down if we don't get away now," Riley said evenly. All fear and anger had left him. He was resigned to their fate. She wasn't. The water reached her waist.

"Where do we go?" Robin asked.

Riley pushed wet hair away from his face. "I don't know. We're a league from the fort."

Could Robin swim upstream for three miles? The deck fell away from her feet. Robin dove to the side, off where the rail had been, swimming away from the deck to safety from the suction. She wouldn't have a choice now. Robin surfaced, turned around, and treaded water. Riley wasn't behind her.

"Riley!"

She spun, searching for him, fighting the weight of her purse and awkward clothes. "Riley!"

He was gone.

Robin dove under the water and opened her eyes. The coming dawn sprayed light, illuminating the clear waters below. The *Angelfish* had stopped sinking. It sat in about fifteen feet of water, the keel forcing the ship to tilt severely onto the sand bed beneath. Silt billowed slowly around it, but Robin found Riley, gripping a mast angled about seven feet below the surface. He was trying to climb to the surface.

Robin swam over to him. She grabbed his arm and pulled, kicking with all her might. He was like dead weight, but she moved her burning legs, because she had no other choice. Breaking the surface, she gasped. Riley took a breath before they were pulled back down. His clothing was too heavy. She maneuvered to his boots and removed them. Then she pulled his fancy coat off. With that, he was buoyant enough for her to keep him above the water.

Riley gasped again and then started sinking.

He couldn't swim.

And she couldn't keep bringing him back up for breaths. Her strength would only hold out for so long, certainly not for three miles of this, regardless of the dozens of soldiers waiting to arrest them. She had to swim to the warship and hope for mercy.

She dragged him. His arms paddled, helping.

"Kick your feet. One after the other. Keep air in your lungs. You can do this," Robin said between waves splashing at her face. Waves that fought to throw them back against the sheer cliffs.

Panting hard, Robin kicked and pulled, fighting to keep her head above water with the weight of Riley dragging her. She would not quit. Up and down the waves, she fought, closing in on the warship.

With each stroke, she spent more time paddling below the surface than above. The weight was dragging her down too much, but they were so close.

"Hang in there. We're almost there."

Relying on her feet to propel her, she used her arm to reach for the ship's ladder. Farther and farther she pushed, and finally her hand gripped the slick wood.

"Grab it. Take it," she ordered, pulling him within range and panting.

Riley gripped the wood and pulled himself free of the water. He coughed and gasped and dashed water from his face. "Why did you bring us here?"

"Where else was there?" she asked.

Riley offered his hand and pulled her onto the ladder next to him. "I don't know, but we can't stay here."

"*Usted!*" an angry voice from above shouted down.

Riley and Robin craned their heads.

"Do you speak Spanish?" Riley asked.

"A little."

"*Sube aquí de inmediato, o disparamos.*" The soldier pointed down at them.

"I didn't understand any of that, but I have a feeling he wants us to climb," Riley said.

"Climb or they'll shoot," Robin said.

"Thank you," Riley said breathlessly, too dramatic for the simple translation. His brows tilted with appreciation, but the lack of worry concerned her most. "Thank you for saving me in more ways than you can imagine."

"Oh, no, you don't," Robin said, reading between the lines. "This isn't goodbye. We'll figure out something."

His hand cupped her jaw. "I admire your optimism, but I'm afraid it's misplaced." His lips found hers and desperation poured through him. A kiss goodbye.

Emotion squeezed her throat, and her lips shifted with sobs. Robin pulled back. "This isn't goodbye. I won't allow it."

"*¡Último aviso! Cinco...cuatro...tres,*" the voice said.

"That I recognize. It's a countdown," Riley said, standing and climbing. "Follow me."

Robin climbed the wet ledges behind Riley. Splashes behind her turned her head. More men were swimming to the warship. At least they weren't alone.

Falling over the rail with a mixture of relief and fear, Robin was circled by soldiers in uniform with muskets outfitted with bayonets at the ready. Robin lifted her palms in surrender. Riley did the same.

Through a break in the soldiers, a man dressed in a higher fashion than the remaining men approached. *Capitán* Delgado, she expected.

More men clambered over the rail behind her and Riley. First Buckley, then Cantu and McKee. Two more men she hadn't met appeared next, but she'd seen them working in the rigging.

All their hands reached skyward too.

Capitán Delgado stopped, hands casually fastening in front of him. His eyes tracked over the newcomers with unreadable features on his thin, lined face. His English was heavily accented. "I know not who you are, but I know that ship. That was my prize stolen by Captain Henry Price. Is he among you?"

"No," Riley said, taking the lead for his remaining men.

Another man dropped over the rail. William Price. He lifted his hands in surrender.

A smug smile lifted Delgado's lips at the news. "He is perished then?"

"No," Riley repeated.

Delgado's features darkened. "We misunderstand. Captain Henry Price is dead?"

William stepped forward. "He might as well be. He's married."

Delgado frowned and stepped closer to Price. "Your attitude is familiar. We've met, have we not?"

"I'm sure I would remember such an ugly mug, like the ass end of a dog."

Delgado visibly shook with contained rage. "I insist a miscommunication between us, correct?"

Price shrugged.

"Which among you is the leader?" Delgado said.

Riley stepped forward, but not without Robin's grip holding him tightly.

Capitán Delgado sized up Riley. "How did you come to own my prize?"

Robin checked the crew around her. Each moved hands to the hits of their weapons. She stuck her hand in her purse. The accuracy rate of those primitive Spanish weapons was not great, but at this range, they wouldn't need to be. Question was, did the antique pistols of the crew work after being submerged?

Her Glock did, and she'd rather fight and die than stand here, waiting to be slaughtered.

Delgado's keen eyes tracked their movements. He stepped back at once. "Stop now, or you'll all be killed."

The pirates exchanged glances, and Riley gestured to stop them.

With a smirk, Delgado said, "To the hold. All of them. A la bodega, todos ellos."

The muskets were lowered, and the survivors were collected with tight grips on their upper arms. A firm grip wrenched Robin's hand from Riley's. He faced her with a look of sorrow that broke her heart. One by one, they were forced below deck.

This ship, although larger, wasn't much nicer than the *Angelfish*. While her eyes were adjusting, Robin tripped on debris strewn on the floor. Her hands landed on a board, and she tried to rub the musk of rotten fish and urine off her scratched palms, but no luck. At the end of the open deck, they were led into a narrow corridor that opened wide. Iron bars crossed the space. The brig. A jail.

Swallowing a thick lump in her throat, Robin, Riley, and the crew were shoved inside, and the gate screamed as it was dragged shut.

The soldiers left them alone.

Robin rushed to Riley's side, and he embraced her.

"Well, what a bugger to be back in here," William Price said, sitting down with his back against the bulwark.

"At least they didn't chain us to the wall," Buckley said, joining him.

"True," Price said. "I admit, the company is more agreeable this time around."

"There's not much we can do now," McKee said. "This warship is crawling with armed soldiers. We have a dozen useless pistols and half a dozen cutlasses between us."

That answered that question. Their pistols were paperweights.

"And we're locked behind bars," Cantu said, sitting on the other side of Price.

"Even if we escaped this ship, where are we going to go? The fort won't welcome us," Hodgens said, joining them.

"I daresay Hodgens is right," Giles added.

"And most of the crew is lost," Cantu said solemnly. "Randall, Vallo, Green, Watts, Gunner, Bauer…"

"I can't shed a tear for Vallo or Green, but you're right, Cantu. This is hopeless. We shouldn't have come for the treasure," Karl said. "Even if the tide rolls out, and we somehow patch the damage to the ship, we lost the mast. There's no coming back from that."

"Assuming we can escape," Giles said solemnly.

"A stupid gamble," Buckley said, sitting against the wall and leaning back. "And after all we survived, Spain's noose will be the end of us. A damned shame. A horrible nightmare. We pressed our luck one too many times. I just hope it's fast, and they do right by our bodies."

Captain Riley pulled away from her embrace. He gazed into her eyes to emphasize his seriousness. "You heard them. You must go."

The remaining crew all lined up on the floor like prisoners awaiting death row. Resigned. The fight had left, but they stared at her with curiosity.

"I can't. I threw my necklace," she said.

Riley reached behind the layers of his wet clothing and pulled the necklace off his head. He placed it in the palm of her hand. "Go."

Tears sprung to her eyes. How could he ask this of her? Leaving now meant he would die. She couldn't live with herself if she couldn't save him. Robin shook her head.

"Go now, I insist. We cannot survive this. I can't let you die when you don't have to." Riley's eyes shimmered with pain, and he sniffled.

"I...I can't go. You're still not safe."

Riley shook her shoulders, anger and tears sending the painful words pouring from his desperate lips. "Your mother's death wasn't your fault, and your colleague's wasn't either. None of this is your fault. You can't save everyone. Understand? You can't. And certainly not us."

Robin sobbed and looked at the amethyst in her palm. Slipping it over her head meant she could go home. What did she have back home for her to return to? Her mom had been murdered. Her father had never been in her life. She'd quit her job. Her apartment was cold and quiet. All she had were Emily Porter and Angela Foxe, but they loved each other, and although they would miss her, they would cry, and eventually they'd move on.

All she wanted was here—Captain Noah Riley. She wouldn't leave him. Not like this. Gripping the necklace tight she flung it away.

But Riley caught it before it went through the bars. In a flash, he opened the chain and pushed it over her head.

Chapter 26

Riley sniffled with relief. Robin was finally safe. He was going to miss her terribly, but the bright side was his pain wouldn't last long. Delgado's hatred ran deep, and his patience had been thin for a long time. Riley dashed the flowing tears from his eyes, no longer concerned over his crew's judgment. Buckley and McKee approached and patted him on the back in support.

"If it's any consolation, I think getting married is a terrible idea," William Price said casually.

The three of them glared at Price.

"What? Think of it—one woman for the rest of your days? One who is always there. Takes up half your sheets. Nags about the laundry. What's so bloody wonderful about that?"

"Says the man whose only experience with women came with a menu," McKee said. "Those negative factors are not negatives at all once you know what married life is like."

"Were you married?" Price asked, skeptical.

"My brother is," McKee said, "and he says it's the greatest thing ever."

"Was his wife nearby when he said it?" Price asked.

McKee paused, thoughts visible on his face. "Well, yea."

Price smiled in self-satisfaction. "Then that means he would've hidden his honesty. Getting in trouble with the missus, I have experience with, and a man will do anything to avoid it."

"Are you telling us Henry is miserable? Your own brother?" Cantu asked.

Price shrugged. "The man has a record for doing foolish things. His case is not a valid point."

Buckley chuckled. "Marrying is not for me either. I love my freedom, but if this was how my life was going to end, in a prison cell with you lot, I think I'd take a warm bed and a naked woman instead, even if she complains about the laundry."

"I'm married," Hodgens said quietly.

Everyone's brows rose.

"You never mentioned her," McKee said.

"No one asked."

That explained why he declined to partake at the brothel.

"What about you, Riley? You're awfully quiet over there," Price said with a sly grin.

Riley raked a hand through his sticky locks. A wistful smile tugged at his lips. "Pretending to be married was both the hardest and easier thing I've ever done. Easiest because Robin was simply perfection. The dawn of my morning, the ray of sunshine in my day, the sensual radiance of my nights. But having to say goodbye, having the swallow the fact that it was fake... I don't know if I'll recover."

"Regular poet over here." Price scoffed, but with a tone of playfulness.

McKee and Cantu made noises of happiness, and heat rose on Riley's throat and cheeks.

Footsteps approached, and all heads turned. More crew were brought down and shoved into the cell. Riley acknowledged each man and watched the soldiers retreat. The *Angelfish* survivors numbered a dozen—fifteen—survivors. A grim total which mattered not at all, since in turn, they'd all be hung.

Captain Riley greeted each man—each man who knew how to swim.

More footsteps approached. If they could get their numbers high enough, there was a chance to fight back. Hopeful, Riley maneuvered through his growing crowd and gripped the iron bars.

Vallo.

And he was unaccompanied.

Riley squeezed the cold iron until his knuckles blanched. "Why am I not surprised?"

The rest of the crew filled in around him. The murmurs began as they realized they'd elected a traitor as the quartermaster.

Vallo smirked. "I outright showed you who I was, but you gave me the benefit of the doubt. For that you are either too trusting or simply foolish. Since you pulled off the raid on Fort James, I've been leaning toward the former. And now that mistake will cost you and your crew a trip to gallows, where you belong," Vallo added.

Riley gritted his teeth. "Let me out and fight me. A proper challenge. A duel of swords. Then we'll see who belongs where."

Vallo laughed. "Unlike you cretins, I don't follow any rules or codes. I do what I must, a pure survival instinct, which clearly you lack."

Riley shook the bars and roared uselessly. Men around him drew their swords as a visual threat.

Vallo stepped back, a broad grin splitting his face. The traitor turned away and said over his shoulder, "Next time I see you, I'll wave to your swinging body."

Riley hit the bars with his open palm, frustration on the verge of breaking him. "If only we could get out of here. I don't care if we can't take them all. I want Vallo. Let me kill Vallo, that traitorous snake."

The previous captain, Henry Price, had warned Riley about Vallo. Although he took the man's warnings seriously, the traitor hadn't shown any sign he'd returned to his devious ways once on board, and Riley had been desperate for knowledgeable hands on deck.

Now he and the crew were paying for it.

"If only we could escape." William Price rubbed at his jaw. "I did get out of here once. Why not again?"

Everyone watched the armorer pull a pin from his pocket. "A woman gave me this handy tool, and since it worked last time, I was inclined to hold on to it. Surely she's forgiven my thievery by now." He climbed to his feet and pushed the pin into the lock, working the tumblers with the tip of his tongue sticking out. One by one, he lined them up, and the gate swung free with a loud squeak.

"They would've heard that," Riley said. "We must be swift. Single file, swords and pistols at the ready, but don't count on your shot working if it's still wet. When we get to the main deck, spread out. I'm going for Vallo first."

"I want Delgado," Price said darkly.

"Everyone else is fair game," Riley added. "It's been an honor sailing with you fine men. Just know whatever happens, I have no regrets."

Especially not about Robin. He wanted to be with her more than anything, but he couldn't stomach her joining him in this fight—one he knew was lost before it began.

ROBIN BLINKED. TWICE. THREE times. Something was wrong with her eyes. She turned in place. The festival. She was at the Tall Ships festival, surrounded by people enjoying themselves. Under her feet was grass. Robin sunk to her knees and touched the green blades. It was real, wasn't it? This was real?

"Hey, lady, nice outfit. Where'd you get it?"

Robin looked up and shielded her eyes from the sun. A man with admiring eyes wearing a polyester bagged costume and an imitation hat stood before her, holding a disposable soft drink. He carefully admired her worn—authentic—dress.

She really had been in the past. It was all real. The sexy captain, the magic necklace, the fort's raid of silver and wine, the sinking *Angelfish*, their capture by the Spanish captain.

But now she was here. Alone.

"Lady?"

Robin stood and dusted off her knees. "I...I made it."

The stranger smiled. "Awesome work. Looks real."

"Thanks."

He sipped from the straw and walked off.

Where were Emily and Angela? Robin dug in her purse and checked her phone. The screen was black. Saltwater fried it—before or after the battery died? Didn't matter. She dropped it back in and scanned the grounds for familiar faces. None. Her friends weren't here.

Robin dug back into the crusty layers of her ruined purse and fisted her keys. She climbed the small hill to the parking lot, desperate for a shower. Her fob didn't work. With a sigh, Robin manually unlocked her car, started it up, and drove home with shaky hands.

Dropping her purse on the coffee table, Robin stripped away the salty rough layers as she walked to the bathroom. She removed the necklace and set it on the sink vanity. In the mirror, her face was drawn with worry. Lines creased the corners of her eyes. Dirt smudged her face. She looked like she got lost camping for weeks. Felt like it, too.

Robin turned on the water, waited for the heat to reach her fingers, and fired up the shower head. She ducked inside and groaned with hot water gliding down her sore body. For several minutes she stood there, water washing away all evidence of...Captain Noah Riley.

The man, who'd appeared on the festival grounds as a disheveled homeless man in the throes of a mental breakdown, turned out to be a man who'd traveled three hundred years into the future. Robin's lips lifted at the memory. If that happened to her, she'd panic just the same.

But she went to the past. Where the panicked homeless man was a leader of a crew of thieves who respected none other than their captain and quartermaster and the rules they agreed to live by. And yet, Riley was still sweet, thoughtful, and more capable of having a heart than most men she'd met.

And they were two worlds apart.

Robin lathered up and paused. Around her finger was Riley's gold ring. His fake proposal for his fake marriage. Tears filled her eyes, but in the privacy of her shower, she didn't care. Sobbing, Robin washed her hair and body.

After turning off the water, drying herself, and getting dressed—in a fresh pair of skinny jeans and a clean T-shirt, she stopped at her mom's photo. She missed her mom. Robin touched the frame, and the gold ring around her finger glinted.

Riley's words returned to her mind. *Your mother's death wasn't your fault.* Robin smiled. He was right. He helped her through the painful truth, to see what she'd been afraid to see. The burglar was to blame for her mom's death, and the bank shooter killed Officer Clark Thompson. Robin wasn't the one hurting people, regardless of her ability to act.

Riley was amazing.

With a sad smile, Robin lifted the frame and sat on the bed. "Hi, Mom. I'm sorry I couldn't save you." She sniffled and sighed, pushing the words out with all her might. "I was young and scared, but it wasn't me who hurt you. A stupid, selfish act by a complete stranger took you from me. You motivated me to do better, to be better. I am who I am because of you, even if it took the encouragement of a...pirate to help me see it." Robin's lips lifted gently. "You'll always live on in my heart, but I have to let you go. I love you."

She set the frame back on her end table and rubbed her thumb along the tiny urn. All goodbyes, no matter how late they were, still hurt.

Robin stood and collected a clean purse from her closet and took another handful of spare magazines. From the crusty purse, she tossed her useless phone away and inspected her Glock. Damp, but still fully functional. Extra magazines intact. She transferred her useful weapons into her clean purse.

In the bathroom, she took a spare roll of toilet paper and her menstrual cup and crammed them in next. With a smirk to herself in the mirror, she gripped the magic necklace.

Riley was right about everything.

Except she was going to save him, because her test wasn't complete, and she loved that stubborn man with an amazing tongue.

Robin slipped the necklace over her head.

Chapter 27

RILEY ROSE HIGH ENOUGH on the final ladder of the warship to see what awaited grim scene they were headed into. He held his fist in the air, ready to signal the fateful charge.

He counted approximately two dozen on the deck performing various duties. A pair of soldiers were setting up what was meant to be a gallows over the boom. Captain Price had told Riley the details of their previous battle with Delgado. It appeared the Spaniard captain intended to finish the task he'd begun all that time ago.

Vallo sat in a chair, the enemy captain's pet, watching the construction and assembly of the gallows.

Captain Riley gritted his teeth.

Capitán Delgado was issuing orders to a man with a pad of papers. The soldiers appeared busy, distracted, and now was their best chance. Riley whispered to himself, picturing Robin's radiant smile, "Someday, in another life, we shall be together again. I will be waiting."

Riley signaled.

He went first, as silent as possible to give all his men the best chance to fight back before the slaughter began. When the soldiers turned their attention, he yelled a startling battle charge. The rest of the crew chimed in, attempting to distract and disorient the soldiers further.

Delgado shouted his own orders and swords clashed. Pistols fired. Clouds of gunpowder obscured the deck.

Riley headed straight to Vallo, whose face turned a shade of ashen. The man stood, drew his own sword and parried Riley's vicious downward swing. Vallo gritted his teeth under the strain, and Riley gritted his teeth against the agony of his injured shoulder.

"You think you're so witty," Vallo said.

"Not witty. Determined to seek justice."

At once, Vallo fell backward and rolled, and Riley stumbled forward from the surprising loss of resistance. The traitor leaped to his feet, smirked, and circled.

Vallo wasn't going to be an easy opponent.

IN THE BLINK OF an eye, Robin returned to the *Peibo del ler San Francisco*, exactly where she'd left: inside the prison cell bars.

But the cell was empty, and the gate stood open.

Had they already been taken for hanging?

How much time had passed?

Robin rushed across the deck, retracing her previous steps when the soldier had brought her down here. She was only going to sneak a look above deck. If at any point the crew was gone and the soldiers were around, she'd use the necklace's power one final time, and somehow survive in a world without Riley.

Choking back that terrible thought, Robin gripped the ladder leading to the main deck. She exhaled a deep breath to prepare herself for what could be her worst nightmare. Gunshots and clashing swords pulled her from the gruesome visual. Robin popped her head up to find the gruesome visual was real.

Pirates were down.

Too many.

The *Angelfish* crew was going to lose, but where was Riley?

Robin climbed up and retrieved her loaded Glock. Men fought all around her, so distracted and busy, none bothered her—if they noticed at all. Robin leveled her Glock, cupping it with both hands. Her hands shook while she searched the carnage for Riley.

Near the stern, Riley was engaged with one of his own crew. Both men were sliced and bleeding. They panted heavily. Vallo—she remembered, who'd been nice to her—stepped forward with his sword raised. Riley stepped back and tripped on a body. He went down. Vallo was going to kill Riley.

Why hadn't Robin been able to squeeze the trigger before? She couldn't choose to end a person's life during a deep spiral, a cry for help. In her mind, she'd always justified the bad guys' behavior, pitied them even. As if a lightbulb flicked on in her mind, Robin figured out the secret. Who needed a department shrink when you had a pirate captain whose life was always hanging in the balance?

As Riley had explained, her mom's and her colleague's deaths weren't her fault. The home invader and Mr. Sean Coulder were at fault. Their actions directly led to their own deaths, and they weren't to be pitied. Their actions weren't to be justified.

Instead of focusing on whether she could be judge, jury, or executioner, she needed to focus on the innocent. Robin would do whatever it took to save those she cared about...to save the man she loved. Because Robin could not live in a world without Captain Noah Riley.

This time, failure was not an option. Robin was not jelly.

Robin aimed her Glock, hands calming down. She moved the barrel until the traitor was between her sights. Robin took up the trigger slack. Breathe in. Breathe out. Now or never. This wasn't a judgment call on a stranger; she was protecting the man she loved. Tensing her arms, she squeezed off a round right between his eyes.

Vallo fell like a wet sponge. Robin rushed over to Riley, who searched the area with surprise.

She kneeled beside him. "Are you okay?"

Riley locked eyes with her. "What are you doing here? I sent you away. For your own good I need you to live."

Robin smiled. "Likewise."

"What killed Vallo?"

Robin waved her Glock.

"That thing works?" Riley asked.

"It does. Do you want me to help the crew or sit here and chat?"

"Do what you can, because otherwise, we're going to lose." Riley climbed to his feet and shook out his shoulders.

Whatever wounds Riley had needed to wait. "Stay here for a minute. Please?" she begged.

Riley still panted from his fight. He nodded, likely happy for a moment's rest before engaging again.

Robin lifted the gun and repeated her relaxing mantra. Breathe in. Breathe out. Now or never. This time, she only pictured Riley's smiling face. She did this for him.

Aiming at each enemy attacking her allies, she squeezed off round after round. Between the eyes. Center of the chest. A couple she had to aim for a thigh but injured was better than not.

Out of ammo. Robin ejected the mag and reloaded. *Pop, pop, pop.* Again and again until she emptied another. And another. Empty mags rattled to the deck.

Robin swiveled her sight, dropping every enemy soldier on the deck.

She paused at the Spaniard captain, whose wide, worried eyes scanned the deck.

Pirates panted, relaxed their swords, and stared at her with wild eyes.

"I'd like one of those," Riley said, gesturing to her gun. "The accuracy is impressive."

Robin pressed her lips together and said dryly, "Yes, the weapon has precision aiming. Do you want me to take out that guy, too?"

Capitán Delgado raised his hands. He was the only Spaniard left standing. A couple injured men groaned on the deck. Bodies littered the surface from both sides.

Riley gently pressed her barrel down. "Let me handle him."

Robin nodded, and Riley crossed the deck. He paused halfway and took something off a man and put it in his mouth. A whistle. He blew long and hard, signaling the battle had ended. Was he telling the other pirates the ship was safe?

Riley reached the enemy captain. Robin trained her Glock on him, just in case.

An injured man nearby climbed to his feet and rushed Riley.

28

Chapter 28

RILEY COULDN'T BELIEVE ROBIN was able to beat an entire company of Spaniard soldiers single-handedly. If he hadn't seen it with his own eyes, he'd never believe it. Only now did he believe Henry Price's story about Angela's feats.

Riley owed Robin endless praise and appreciation. First, for too long *Capitán* Delgado had plagued Riley's crew, and after all this time, Riley was going to end it.

"Courtesy of one happily retired Captain Henry Price," Riley said, and reeled his arm back for the fatal strike.

Delgado curled up on the deck, covering his head in fear, but a hand blocked Riley's attack.

"I've been fighting this weasel since the battle began. I'm not giving up now," William Price said, wiping blood from his mouth and breathing heavily.

Riley nodded. "If you should fail, fear not. Robin will level him as she did all the other enemies on board."

Price looked around, as if seeing the battle's end for the first time. His eyes opened wide. "She did this?"

"Yea."

Delgado, unarmed, glanced between them as they conversed, as if deciding who the fatal attack would come from, but with no soldiers to back him up, he was too afraid to make a move.

Price lowered a hand on Riley's undamaged shoulder. "This once, I suppose I retract my statement of marriage. She's as fearless and strong as any other pirate. If I had to choose a woman, one like her would satisfy my whims. Don't let that one get away."

"Or what? You'll scoop her up from under me?"

William Price snorted a laugh. "Now don't be ridiculous. I gave you words of encouragement; I'm firm on my bachelorhood remaining intact." Price crossed himself in prayer.

"I thought you didn't believe," Riley said, amused at his movements from head to heart and shoulder to shoulder.

"When serious matters threaten one's livelihood, one can never be too careful."

Riley laughed and glanced over his shoulder at Robin, who helped survivors to their feet. Warmth filled his chest. He hoped she'd stay this time.

Price picked up a sword, and Delgado cried out, "Allow me to defend myself in a fair fight."

"You held me prisoner in that hold for months, and you had the gall to try it a second time. There will be no third, and you don't deserve the honor of fairness." Price plunged the sword into the Spaniard's chest, piercing just below the ribcage.

Delgado's mouth dropped open, and his face pinched in pain. He crumpled over, dragging in shallow breaths.

Price threw the sword away and pulled Riley into a hug. Emotion clogged his voice. "It's over. It's finally over."

"Henry would be proud," Riley said, and Price sobbed in his shoulder.

Riley held the broken armorer and caught another glance at Robin. She helped Hodgens to his feet, and the helmsman gestures of rejecting further assistance, assuring her he was fine. She helped Cantu stand next, and the large man pulled Robin into a bear hug. Their appreciation brought tears to Riley's eyes.

More pirates dropped over the rail to the deck and started assisting those who'd fallen.

Where was Buckley?

Riley pulled back from his friend. "He can't harm anyone again. Let's help the others."

William Price nodded and swiped away tears.

ROBIN NO LONGER NEEDED her Glock, which was great, because she only had a couple shots left. She'd found a man moaning nearby, and her instincts to save people reignited. Grateful for her jeans and T-shirt, she nimbly searched the deck for pirates, helping them to their feet, and for those who were too injured to stand, she tore off bits of their clothes to tie knots over bleeding wounds.

In her element, she canvassed the deck, triaging and assisting the downed men. Several who'd been hurt but were still lucid enough to watch the battle unfold offered their thanks for her most unusual weapon. One asked if she was a spy. She assured him she was not, but Robin had a feeling he didn't believe her.

One man lifted a hand for assistance, and Robin kneeled at his side.

Buckley.

"It's over. Anything hurt?" she asked.

He was bleeding all over, and one eye was swollen shut, but with her question, Buckley chuckled. The sound was thick and wet. "Noah Riley christened our new ship the *Angelfish*. I didn't realize an angel would be sent in reward."

His functional eye swept over her modern clothes. "Thank you, angel. Regardless of where that power comes from, thank you so much. I get to say goodbye after an honorable fight to the end, rather than a shameful hanging by the enemy."

A syrupy gasp made Robin wince, and tears stung her eyes.

"And I want you...to tell Riley...he's the best captain a pirate could ask for. Tell Price...to find himself a woman; it's not a terrible way to live. And for you, my dear, thank you for returning to us and saving the crew. I'll never see the future, but I have hope for you all."

Tears flooded Robin's eyelids and slid down her cheeks.

"And Robin?" he added.

She gripped his hand in comfort and he gasped again.

"Marry that man...for real this time."

Robin smiled, and a sob escaped her lips. Buckley gasped again, and his clear eye closed. His chest stilled.

A hand landed on her shoulder, and Robin looked up to see Riley. She set Buckley's hand down on his chest and stood. She fell into Riley's arms, and he hugged her tightly.

"Buckley's gone," she said, sobbing.

Riley didn't answer. He held her until she composed herself. She leaned back and sniffled. "He said you're the best captain he had, and that Price needs to find a woman."

Riley chuckled and sniffled. "Did he say anything else?"

Robin couldn't bring herself to push the captain into something he didn't want. She'd served her purpose. She'd posed as his wife to capture a treasure and saved the crew from the consequences. She didn't fail. Her work was done. Now Riley could tell her to go home to safety, and she had no logical reason to refuse.

"No, he didn't."

"He's a good man, but he's happy now. All he wanted was an end in glory. We're all happy for him."

"What about the *Angelfish*?" Robin asked, pulling out of his arms, and searching the water's shimmering surface.

"It's lost."

Seeing all the bodies pooled on the deck, anger surged through her. "You can't leave that treasure. Too many people died for it. You can't let it sit there and go to waste."

"It's over," he said, holding her hands. "It's finally over."

When she thought of her future, all she could picture was her secure in Riley's arms, but as he said, it was over. She'd fulfilled all but one promise. She'd promised to return home after Riley was safe.

With a shaky deep breath, Robin tugged his ring off her finger. "You can have this back then."

Riley stared at it.

Behind them, bright daylight showed the survivors cleaning up the deck and removing bodies by tossing them over. Blood coated the slick surface. Robin trembled with her receding adrenaline. Only about twenty men survived the sinking and the battle.

"I want you to keep it," Riley said, closing her fingers around it.

"I can't keep your family's ring," Robin said, urging him to take it.

"My wife wears my ring."

Robin stared at him. His eyes glistened with tears, and his lips pulled into a tender smile.

Her mouth opened, but before she could answer, Riley added, "For years I couldn't see a future. I was reckless, foolish, hoping a captain followed a dangerous hunt for the chance to end my life honorably, so I could return to my betrothed—only because I didn't know real happiness. Now I look into the future, and all I see is you. In the same breath you can save my life and kill my enemy. You helped my men when they didn't deserve it. And you returned to me. From the safety of your home, you came back to me. I want you to be my wife."

"I...I..." Robin couldn't catch her breath.

"I love you," Riley said. "I love you so much I can't live without you. Marry me."

Robin removed the magic amethyst from around her neck. She fisted it while Riley watched with worry on his brow. Shades of purple reflected the sunlight, a beautiful gem, simply stunning. Robin sighed. Such a waste. On a deep breath, she heaved the necklace over the rail. It soared and splashed, never to be found again.

Hope reached his eyes, and Robin smiled. "Yes, of course, I'll marry you. For real this time. I love you, Captain Riley."

He took the gold ring from her. With careful hands, he replaced the ring back where it belonged. "It's Noah. You've earned that right, my love, my Robin." Riley beamed and broke into a joyful song and held her hand up as if to begin a dance.

The cleanup crew paused to watch their mini celebration, smiles on their faces, and a few added their voices to the choir.

Riley spun Robin on the deck and dipped her low. "I already got my plunder, and I'm not sharing, but these sea dogs need their money." He winked and straightened her upright. Turning over his shoulder, he hollered, "Let's get that treasure, men!"

Robin laughed, and the crew cheered. Robin was home.

29

Chapter 29

THE WARSHIP, NOW RENAMED the *Neptune*, sailed as close to the *Angelfish* wreck as the draft would allow. The warship's broadside volley had punched massive holes in the hull of their old ship, leaving easy access to the hold. All the survivors on board could swim, except Noah. Most of them took turns collecting a ballast rock, sinking to the treasure chests, and hauling up a handful.

In the meantime, Noah plotted a course, and Giles made dinner. The cook was ecstatic over the Spanish Royalty's galley. And Jack Watts, the new carpenter's mate and Buckley's next in line, managed to survive the sinking. He'd never bothered to climb aboard the warship. Now he fixed the minor holes in *Neptune*'s hull. Surprisingly, the warship was well-stocked with provisions.

Standing before the crew, Captain Noah Riley said, "With recent events, I have decided to step down as your captain. We will head to Hispaniola to allow myself and my wife-to-be to disembark. At which point, you'll need to elect yourselves a new leader. Hodgens, you have your coordinates. Weigh anchor, you sea dogs!" The men scattered to their orders, and Noah added, "Oh, one more thing."

They respectfully stopped to listen.

"If this cabin door is closed, don't open it."

The men laughed and made insinuating calls. Since Robin had saved the crew, all of them accepted her presence.

Wind filled the sails, and the ship moved through the water.

Noah approached her with an open hand. "Come with me."

Robin accepted it and followed him into the cabin, which was much fancier than the *Angelfish*'s. He closed the door behind them and turned to face her. She searched his hungry eyes. Before she could lay a hand on him, his lips stole hers.

Robin caught her breath as they changed positions, and her hands quickly undressed him.

Noah fought with her skinny jeans. Robin chuckled against his lips. "I'll help."

"What blasted material is this? Chastity clothing to keep men away? It certainly works."

Noah watched hungrily as she unbuttoned and unzipped the tight jeans. She wriggled her hips to slide out of the fabric, and Noah pounced on her lips again as if afraid to ever be apart again. She blindly fussed with his tunic, flipping it over his head, and flinging to the floorboards.

Noah's broad hands palmed her torso as he slid her T-shirt up. His fingers paused at her bra. He pulled away from her lips and inspected the lingerie with a sigh. "I say, I like the detail here, but I'd like it even better on the floor."

Robin laughed. "Isn't this easier than corsets or whatever women of this day wore?"

He pulled off her shirt and circled her, assessing her bra. "Indeed. I don't think we need a handmaiden to dress and undress you. I must say I find this smaller undergarment is quite...fetching."

"Quit talking and take it off."

Noah's eyes lit up. "Yes, ma'am. You don't need to ask twice."

He unfastened the hooks at the back, exposing her completely. While he stared, Robin untied his breeches and dropped them to the floor. He stiff cock, along with the rest of her, was happy to see her.

Noah scooped her up and set her on his new bed. "Do you want it fast or slow?"

Robin smiled slyly. "How long until Hispaniola?"

Noah groaned.

Weeks later the Neptune crossed the Atlantic and arrived at a port in Hispaniola. Robin disembarked with Noah Riley at her side, waving goodbye to Boatswain Karl, Giles, Hodgens, Cantu, McKee, Watts, and Price, and many others she hadn't personally met.

After several days, they'd managed to recover two thousand pounds of silver and a few bottles of wine, and since all the troublemakers had perished, Noah asked if the crew wanted to redistribute the silver equally. The survivors agreed unanimously, and no one complained about Noah and Robin each getting a share.

To her, it didn't seem like much, but Noah assured her it was a lifetime's worth of money. After a stop at a bank to deposit their shares, she and Noah took a carriage up a dirt road outside of town.

Besides ample provisions, the warship also had very fine clothing. Robin had dressed in a white and gold lacy top and a glossy-sheened full skirt with decorative green satin, which complemented her red hair perfectly.

Noah had dressed in an ivory tunic, a matching green vest, and to top it off, he wore a gold coat with tails. Brown breeches and an ivory cravat finished the look. He tied his hair back with a gold ribbon. Robin left her locks tumbling over her shoulders and down her back. They looked like royalty. And Robin felt like it.

At the top of a hill overlooking the ocean was a fancy two-story plantation with a sprawling front lawn. It was beautiful.

"Who lives here?" Robin asked, holding his hand. They followed the curving driveway and climbed the porch steps.

"Someone I want you to meet. I sent a message ahead. We won't be the only visitors."

Dinner party with Noah's friends? Robin was excited but very nervous. She didn't know he had any.

Noah knocked on the door, and they were promptly greeted by a woman in a dress, apron, and bonnet. She politely led them inside. The air was the same temperature as outside—hot and humid. Plants were artfully placed around the lobby, and a sparkly candle chandelier hung from the ceiling.

Noah continued bringing her deeper inside like he'd been here before. Through a door to the left, two men sat in fancy upholstered chairs with a detailed carving, facing a fireplace. Noah released her arm and walked toward the two men, who promptly stood with smiles on their faces. Noah hugged each man and faced her, beaming with joy.

Robin didn't recognize them.

Noah gestured for her to come closer. "Robin, I want you to meet Eric and Henry, my two good friends."

Robin smiled and approached. She held out her hand to shake, but each man kissed her knuckles. Sweet, but something she would have to get used to.

Movement out of the corner of her eye caught her attention. Two women in extravagant gowns stood with smiles of their own. Robin squinted. The faces didn't match the clothing.

"Robin!" Angela called.

"You're here!" Emily said, holding out her arms.

Robin stared dumbfounded. She said the first thing that popped into her head, "Neither of you answered my texts."

Her friends laughed and gestured for her to come closer. Robin was embraced by the warmth of her best friends, and she dashed away her tears. Noah was her home, but with her friends, she was whole.

"How did you get here?" Robin asked. "I mean, I know how, but like, how?"

Emily chuckled. "The necklace brought me to the *Sea Lion*, where I met Eric." Catching his name, Eric smiled, bowed, and said a phrase in French. "He thought I was a man most of the time he knew me, but we worked it out." Emily winked at him.

"*Sea Lion* for me too," Angela said, "until it sank, but the new ship had been renamed the *Angelfish* after we left. We were stranded in Cuba for a while. Camping took on a whole new meaning, and I'm perfectly happy to never step foot in sand again."

"Seems like the ship was named after you," Robin noted.

"It was," Henry said, catching his name next. "No one else deserved the honor." Henry gazed lovingly at Angela before returning to the men's conversation.

"What's your story, Robin?" Emily asked.

"I landed on the *Angelfish* and we raided a fort in Africa."

The men's conversation stopped so they could listen.

"We would've got away unscathed had Vallo not told *Capitán* Delgado where we were going."

"That blasted imbecile!" Henry shouted in frustration. "I warned you about Vallo, Riley. I warned you. What damage did the traitor do this time?"

"You did warn me, but he's dead now. So is Delgado. In fact, your dear brother killed Delgado."

"Good for him," Henry said gruffly. "My brother deserved that chance. I presume he lives? What of the soldiers, and the ship?"

"William Price is wealthy, well, and as we speak on his way with the crew back to Nassau, where I expect he will find the bottom of several bottles and a few whores."

Henry made a noise of derision. "That man needs to grow up."

"He's rich now. He can do whatever pleases him," Noah countered. "The crew now owns the *Peibo del ler San Francisco* to continue the account or sell it and break up. I wasn't part of their goings on, and I don't know who they voted to lead next. As much as I care for my fellow men, I have everything I need here." With a wistful smile of pride, Noah added, "Robin killed almost all the soldiers on board."

He exchanged a glance with her, and heat rushed up her cheeks at the praise.

"How?" Eric Lemoine asked, brows raised.

"You brought your Glock, didn't you?" Angela answered for her.

Robin slipped it out of her purse. "I have three rounds left, maybe. It's pretty much useless."

Eric and Henry approached and stared at her gun like it was some zoo animal. They made noises of amazement.

"This took down the entire ship of soldiers?" Henry asked, pointing in wonder.

"Just about," Robin said, taking his appreciation as a compliment of her skills and not the weapon itself.

"Well then, it deserves a place of honor. Mount it above the fireplace," Henry said.

"It's not a trophy," Robin said, putting it back in her purse.

"It is. It truly is," Eric said and sat down with a hand pressed against his forehead.

"The warship is now the *Neptune*, in case you should come across that name," Noah said.

"Who has fallen?" Henry asked, joining his friend in an adjacent chair. Both men appeared overwhelmed with the news.

Robin's friends sat on a couch, dresses splayed around them. Eric gestured for Noah and Robin to sit and join them, and Noah took her hand. They sat on the couch next to each other.

"From the original crew, we lost Buckley. He went down swinging and died a happy man," Noah said.

"Good for him," Eric said. "He found peace."

As did Robin. Peace in knowing a unicorn existed, that there was happiness out there for her, and sometimes things had a way of working out okay. Robin squeezed Noah's hand.

The woman who'd greeted them at the door brought in tea and biscuits. Robin thanked her profusely before her friends educated her on proper etiquette. Getting used to the food would take time, but clearly her friends handled it fine. The clothing was another obstacle altogether. Noah's wild world was foreign to her, but if the only way she could have him was to survive it, she would. She'd do anything for him.

Catching up took hours and promises of regular visits were made on all sides. And Robin intended to keep every one of them. They waved goodbye to their friends, and Robin stopped Noah on the driveway.

She whispered into his ear, "Thank you. You've given me the world, and I love you so much."

Noah beamed with pride. "And if I hadn't met you, I wouldn't be here, so you've given me a reason to live. Let's get out of here."

After a very passionate kiss in full view of the house, they organized a wedding on Hispaniola for their friends to attend. They married, and Robin slept soundly, knowing those she loved were safe and happy.

30

Epilogue

As the Tall Ships festival wound down on a late Sunday evening, customers scattered from the vendor tables. Vendors packed up and took down their tents. The ships were preparing for a voyage to their next port of call, and a cleaning crew picked up the strewn litter.

Chaos strolled the lawn, taking in the sights. Every place he stopped still interested him, even after all these millennia. How humanity changed from one decade to the next was remarkable. How it changed through the centuries was shocking, but still, over the thousands of years, the changes entertained him greatly.

But he lived for it. He was Chaos.

If for no other reason than humanity would suffer worse at the hands of his brother, Order. That was some dystopian dysfunction. The two of them never saw eye-to-eye. So long as Chaos retained his preternatural form, he'd continue the fight to keep humans enjoying the life they chose, and there was no better way than making these silly humans fall in love.

Order hated that.

And Chaos loved it. And when humanity debated the concept of free will, Chaos pulled up a chair and grabbed popcorn.

He arrived at this particular time for a reason. Chaos stopped at a special vendor's table and watched Esther Brumley gather her wares before interrupting. He'd recruited her about ninety years ago. Without him, she would've passed from cancer. Instead, she lived a long life matchmaking couples through time. She appreciated it, because she'd called upon him each year and gifted him a fruit basket. What more could say 'thank you' than that?

"Are we all set then, kid?" Chaos asked his love curator.

Esther's thin, saggy arms dropped to her sides as she looked up and smiled. "Hi, boss. I'm still packing. I need a little more time before I'll be ready for my next assignment."

Chaos checked his watch. "Actually, that's perfect. I need to jump over to Milwaukee, nineteen-eighty-something."

"Recruiting another agent?"

"Kiko Takai. Had her heart torn out. She's going to need, oh...about a hundred years to heal the damage."

"Poor girl."

"Yeah, and she's much younger than I usually prefer, so this meeting could take a while. Good thing you won't notice."

Esther rolled her eyes. "Time jokes never end, do they?"

Chaos chuckled at her criticism and her pun. She was clever. "I'll be back when you're ready."

Esther nodded her understanding, and Chaos disappeared on a blink to find his next agent, currently shuffling through life in despair and cradling a knife in fear.

Chaos was the only one who could help.

He'd seen it.

Amended Special Note:

While the events of this novel are fiction,
the pirate raid on Gambia Castle, *where 2,000
pounds of silver and all the alcohol were taken
without a shot fired*, was real, performed by
Captain Howell Davis in 1718.
Also, the *San Francisco* was a real Spanish
warship that had been captured by pirates and
renamed *Neptune* by Dutch pirate Laurens de
Graaf.

Dear Reader,

THAT'S THE END OF the Pirates in Time series. I hope you loved the swashbuckling adventure as much as I do! Looking for similar but without the pirates? Check out my Matchmaker in Time series. How about vampires? I've got the Immortal Protector series, too. Find them and more at StephanieFlynn.com.

As an indie author, I'm thrilled you decided to share your time with me, exploring the crazy worlds residing in my head and keeping me up at night. Your reviews are very important to me, so if you enjoyed this book, please consider leaving some stars for Robin Hall and Captain Riley's story in Pirate's Plunder **(Pirates in Time Book 3)**.

If you found any typos or errors, I blame my cat. Rat her out at: support@stephanieflynn.com.

Thank you for your support!

Also By Stephanie Flynn

Find my catalog at StephanieFlynn.com

Immortal Protector series

0.5 Vampire's Distraction

1 Vampire's Deception

2 Vampire's Secret

3 Vampire's Promise

3.5 Elf Bound

4 Vampire's Demand

Immortal Protector Side Tales

Deer Holiday

Love Claws

Depths of the Heart

Matchmaker in Time series

0.5 Minutes to Live

1 Seconds to Act
2 Hours to Arrive
3 Days to Hide
4 Years to Savor

Pirates in Time series
1 Pirate's Prize
2 Pirate's Treasure
3 Pirate's Plunder

Time Travel Romance Shorts
Fateful Time
One Crazy Time

If you like your urban fantasy without the romance, too, check out Stephanie Flynn's other name, Marie Flynn!

About Stephanie Flynn

Stephanie Flynn writes action-packed paranormal romance filled with adventure, suspense, and danger. She lives in Michigan, USA, with her husband and kids, and she spends her writing time surrounded by a herd of normal cats who bat everything off her desk, including her coffee. Check out her website for more books: StephanieFlynn.com